Ryan's mouth was warm and skilled, his kiss sending an explosion of light through her brain and fire through her belly.

It should have felt wrong, kissing him. But it felt right—standing here with his lips against hers and nothing around them but the sound and smell of the sea.

Jenna dug her fingers into the front of his wetsuit, felt the hardness of his body brush against her knuckles. The fire spread, licking its way through her limbs until she was unsteady on her feet, and his grip on her tightened, his mouth more demanding as they kissed hungrily, feasting, exploring, discovering.

Then Rebel barked.

Ryan lifted his mouth from hers, his reluctance evident in the time he took. Dazed and disorientated, Jenna stared up at him for a moment, and then at his mouth.

Rebel barked again, and she turned her head, trying to focus on the dog.

'People on the beach.' His voice was calm and steady. 'Clearly we're not the only early risers.'

'Obviously not.' She knew she sounded stilted but she had no idea what to say. Were they supposed to talk about it? Or pretend it had never happened? 'I should be getting home. Lexi will be waking up...' Feeling really strange, she lifted a shaking hand to her forehead. The ___ everything. Her world had tilted.

Dear Reader

Four years ago I wrote two books based on the fictitious Scottish island of Glenmore. I enjoyed writing them so much and had such enthusiastic feedback from readers that I wrote a third—THE REBEL DOCTOR'S BRIDE.

This summer I decided to return there again. Jenna is a single mother who moves to Glenmore intent on building a new life for herself and her teenage daughter. Bruised and still in shock after discovering her husband's infidelities, the last thing she is looking for is love. Dr Ryan McKinley isn't looking for love either. But the people who live in the tight-knit community of Glenmore have other ideas, and Jenna discovers once again that life doesn't always turn out according to plan. Like all mothers, she has to juggle numerous demands on her time and her emotional energy. She is so used to putting herself second that she has never really allowed herself to consider her own needs. Until now.

Glenmore and its inhabitants are so familiar to me that setting a story there is like returning to a beloved holiday destination. Writing this book allowed me to explore so many aspects of living and working in a small island community. I loved giving Jenna her much deserved happy ending, and I hope you enjoy reading her story as much as I enjoyed writing it.

I love hearing from my readers. Your kind, generous and enthusiastic feedback is what keeps my hands on my keyboard! You can contact me via my website at www.sarahmorgan.com, and find me on Facebook and Twitter.

Warmest wishes

Sarah

xx

DARE SHE DATE
THE DREAMY DOC?

BY
SARAH MORGAN

First published in Great Britain 2010
Harlequin Mills & Boon Limited,
Eton House, 18-24 Paradise Road, Richmond, Surrey TW9 1SR

© Sarah Morgan 2010

ISBN: 978 0 263 21387 4

Harlequin Mills & Boon [...] that are natural,
renewable and recyclable products and made from wood grown in
sustainable forests. The logging and manufacturing process conform
to the legal environmental [...] country of origin.

Printed and bound in Great Britain
by CPI Antony Rowe, Chippenham, Wiltshire

Sarah Morgan is a British writer who regularly tops the bestseller lists with her lively stories for both Mills & Boon® Medical™ Romance and Modern™ Romance. As a child Sarah dreamed of being a writer, and although she took a few interesting detours on the way she is now living that dream. She firmly believes that reading romance is one of the most satisfying and fat-free escapist pleasures available. Her stories are unashamedly optimistic, and she is always pleased when she receives letters from readers saying that her books have helped them through hard times. *RT Book Reviews* has described her writing as 'action-packed and sexy'.

Sarah lives near London with her husband and two children, who innocently provide an endless supply of authentic dialogue. When she isn't writing or nagging about homework Sarah enjoys music, movies, and any activity that takes her outdoors.

To all the readers
who asked me to write another book set on Glenmore.

CHAPTER ONE

'I CAN'T believe you've dragged me to the middle of nowhere.
You must really hate me.' The girl slumped against the rail of
the ferry, sullen and defiant, every muscle in her slender
teenage frame straining with injured martyrdom and simmer-
ing rebellion.

Jenna dragged her gaze from the misty beauty of the approaching island and focused on her daughter. 'I don't hate
you, Lexi,' she said quietly. 'I love you. Very much.'

'If you loved me, we'd still be in London.'

Guilt mingled with stress and tension until the whole in-
digestible mix sat like a hard ball behind her ribs. 'I thought
this was the best thing.'

'Best for you, maybe. Not me.'

'It's a fresh start. A new life.' As far away from her old life
as possible. Far away from everything that reminded her of
her marriage. Far away from the pitying glances of people
she'd used to think were her friends.

'I liked my old life!'

So had she. Until she'd discovered that her life had been a
lie. They always said you didn't know what was going on in
someone else's marriage—she hadn't known what was going
on in her own.

Jenna blinked rapidly, holding herself together through

will-power alone, frightened by how bad she felt. Not for the first time, she wondered whether eventually she was going to crack. People said that time healed, but how much time? Five years? Ten years? Certainly not a year. She didn't feel any better now than she had when it had first happened. She was starting to wonder whether some things just didn't heal— whether she'd have to put on the 'everything is OK' act for the rest of her life.

She must have been doing a reasonably good job of convincing everyone she was all right because Lexi was glaring at her, apparently oblivious to her mother's own personal struggle. 'You had a perfectly good job in London. We could have stayed there.'

'London is expensive.'

'So? Make Dad pay maintenance or something. He's the one who walked out.'

The comment was like a slap in the face. 'I don't want to live off your father. I'd rather be independent.' Which was just as well, Jenna thought bleakly, given Clive's reluctance to part with any money for his daughter. 'Up here there are no travel costs, you can go to the local school, and they give me a cottage with the job.'

That was the best part. A cottage. Somewhere that was their own. She wasn't going to wake up one morning and find it had been taken away from them.

'How can you be so calm and civilised about all this?' Lexi looked at her in exasperation. 'You should be angry. I tell you now, if a man ever treats me the way Dad treated you I'll punch his teeth down his throat and then I'll take a knife to his—'

'Lexi!'

'Well, I would!'

Jenna took a slow deep breath. 'Of course I've felt angry. And upset. But what's happened has happened, and we have to get on with it.' Step by step. Day by day.

'So Dad's left living in luxury with his new woman and we're exiled to a remote island that doesn't even have electricity? Great.'

'Glenmore is a wonderful place. Keep an open mind. I loved it when I was your age and I came with my grandparents.'

'People *choose* to come here?' Lexi glared at the rocky shore, as if hoping to scare the island into vanishing. 'Is this seriously where you came on holiday? That's totally tragic. You should have sued them for cruelty.'

'I loved it. It was a proper holiday. The sort where we spent time together—' Memories swamped her and suddenly Jenna was a child again, excited at the prospect of a holiday with her grandparents. Here—and perhaps only here—she'd felt loved and accepted for who she was. 'We used to make sandcastles and hunt for shells on the beach—'

'Wow. I'm surprised you didn't die of excitement.'

Faced with the sting of teenage sarcasm, Jenna blinked. Suddenly she wished she were a child again, with no worries. No one depending on her. Oh, for crying out loud—she pushed her hair away from her eyes and reminded herself that she was thirty-three, not twelve. 'It *is* exciting here. Lexi, this island was occupied by Celts and Vikings—it's full of history. There's an archaeological dig going on this summer and they had a small number of places for interested teenagers. I've booked you on it.'

'You *what*?' Appalled, Lexi lost her look of martyred boredom and shot upright in full defensive mode. 'I am not an interested teenager so you can count me out!'

'Try it, Lexi,' Jenna urged, wondering with a lurch of horror what she was going to do if Lexi refused to co-operate. 'You used to love history when you were younger, and—'

'I'm not a kid any more, Mum! This is my summer holiday. I'm supposed to have a rest from school. I don't want to be taught history!'

Forcing herself to stay calm, Jenna took a slow, deep breath; one of the many she'd taken since her daughter had morphed from sweet child to scary teen. When you read the pregnancy books, why didn't it warn you that the pain of being a mother didn't end with labour?

Across the ferry she caught sight of a family, gathered together by the rail. Mother, father, two children—they were laughing and talking, and Jenna looked away quickly because she'd discovered that nothing was more painful than being around happy families when your own was in trouble.

Swallowing hard, she reminded herself that not every modern family had perfect symmetry. Single-parent families, stepfamilies—they came in different shapes. Yes, her family had been broken, but breakages could be mended. They might heal in a different shape, but they could still be sturdy.

'I thought maybe we could go fishing.' It was up to her to be the glue. It was up to her to knit her family together again in a new shape. 'There's nothing quite like eating a fish you've caught yourself.'

Lexi rolled her eyes and exhaled dramatically. 'Call me boring, but gutting a fish with my mother is *so* not my idea of fun. Stop trying so hard, Mum. Just admit that the situation is crap.'

'Don't swear, Alexandra.'

'Why not? Grandma isn't around to hear and it *is* crap. If you want my honest opinion, I hope Dad and his shiny new girlfriend drown in their stupid hot tub.'

Relieved that no one was standing near them, Jenna rubbed her fingers over her forehead, reminding herself that this was not the time to get into an argument. 'Let's talk about us for a moment, not Dad. There are six weeks of summer holiday left before term starts. I'm going to be working, and I'm not leaving you on your own all day. That's why I thought archae-ology camp would be fun.'

'About as much fun as pulling my toenails out one by one. I don't need a babysitter. I'm fifteen.'

And you're still a child, Jenna thought wistfully. Underneath that moody, sullen exterior lurked a terrified girl. And she knew all about being terrified, because she was too. She felt like a plant that had been growing happily in one spot for years, only to be dug up and tossed on the compost heap. The only difference between her and Lexi was that she had to hide it. She was the grown-up. She had to look confident and in control.

Not terrified, insecure and needy.

Now that it was just the two of them, Lexi needed her to be strong. But the truth was she didn't feel strong. When she was lying in bed staring into the darkness she had moments of utter panic, wondering whether she could actually do this on her own. Had she been crazy to move so far away? Should she have gone and stayed with her parents? At least that would have eased the financial pressure, and her mother would have been able to watch out for Lexi while she worked. Imagining her mother's tight-lipped disapproval, Jenna shuddered. There were two sins her mother couldn't forgive and she'd committed both of them. No, they were better on their own.

Anger? Oh, yes, she felt anger. Not just for herself, but for Lexi. What had happened to the man who had cradled his daughter when she'd cried and spent weeks choosing exactly the right dolls' house? Jenna grabbed hold of the anger and held it tightly, knowing that it was much easier to live with than misery. Anger drove her forward. Misery left her inert.

She needed anger if she was going to make this work. And she *was* going to make it work.

She had to.

'We're going to be OK. I promise, Lexi.' Jenna stroked a hand over the teenager's rigid shoulder, relieved when her touch wasn't instantly rejected. 'We'll have some fun.'

'Fun is seeing my friends. Fun is my bedroom at home and my computer—'

Jenna didn't point out that they didn't have a home any more. Clive had sold it—the beautiful old Victorian house that she'd tended so lovingly for the past thirteen years. When they'd first married money had been tight, so she'd decorated every room herself…

The enormity of what she'd lost engulfed her again and Jenna drew in a jerky breath, utterly daunted at the prospect of creating a new life from scratch. By herself.

Lexi dug her hand in her pocket and pulled out her mobile phone. 'No signal. Mum, there's no signal!' Panic mingled with disgust as she waved her phone in different directions, trying to make it work. 'I swear, if there's no signal in this place I'm swimming home. It's bad enough not seeing my friends, but not talking to them either is going to be the end.'

Not by herself, Jenna thought. With her daughter. Somehow they needed to rediscover the bond they'd shared before the stability of their family had been blown apart.

'This is a great opportunity to try a few different things. Develop some new interests.'

Lexi gave her a pitying look. 'I already have interests, Mum. Boys, my friends, hanging out, and did I say boys? Chatting on my phone—boys. Normal stuff, you know? No, I'm sure you don't know—you're too old.' She huffed moodily. 'You met Dad when you were sixteen, don't forget.'

Jenna flinched. She had just managed to put Clive out of her mind and Lexi had stuffed him back in her face. And she wasn't allowed to say that she'd had no judgement at sixteen. She couldn't say that the whole thing had been a mistake, because then Lexi would think she was a mistake and that wasn't true.

'All I'm asking is that you keep an open mind while you're here, Lexi. You'll make new friends.'

'Anyone who chooses to spend their life in a place like this is seriously tragic and no friend of mine. Face it, Mum, basically I'm going to have a miserable, lonely summer and it's all your fault.' Lexi scowled furiously at the phone. 'There's still no signal. I hate this place.'

'It's probably something to do with the rocky coastline. It will be fine once we land on the island.'

'It is not going to be fine! Nothing about this place is fine.' Lexi stuffed the phone moodily back in her pocket. 'Why didn't you let me spend the summer with Dad? At least I could have seen my friends.'

Banking down the hurt, Jenna fished for a tactful answer. 'Dad is working,' she said, hoping her voice didn't sound too robotic. 'He was worried you'd be on your own too much.' Well, what was she supposed to say? Sorry, Lexi, your dad is selfish and wants to forget he has responsibilities so he can spend his summer having sex with his new girlfriend.

'I wouldn't have cared if Dad was working. I could have hung around the house. I get on all right with Suzie. As long as I block out the fact that my Dad is hooked up with someone barely older than me.'

Jenna kept her expression neutral. 'People have relationships, Lexi. It's part of life.' Not part of *her* life, but she wasn't going to think about that now. For now her priorities were remembering to breathe in and out, get up in the morning, go to work, earn a living. Settling into her job, giving her daughter roots and security—that was what mattered.

'When you're young, yes. But he's old enough to know better. They should be banned for everyone over twenty-one.' Lexi shuddered. 'Thank goodness you have more sense. It's a relief you're past all that.'

Jenna blinked. She was thirty-three. Was thirty-three really past it? Perhaps it was. By thirty-three you'd discovered that fairy tales were for children, that men didn't ride up with swords to rescue you; they were more likely to run you down while looking at the pretty girl standing behind you.

Resolutely she blocked that train of thought. She'd promised herself that she wasn't going to do that. She wasn't going to generalise and blame the entire male race for Clive's shortcomings. She wasn't going to grow old bitter and twisted, giving Lexi the impression that all men were selfish losers. It wasn't men who had hurt her; it was Clive. One man—not all men.

It was Clive who had chosen to have a rampant affair with a trainee lawyer barely out of college. It was Clive who had chosen to have sex on his desk without bothering to lock the door. There were moments when Jenna wondered if he'd done it on purpose, in the hope of being caught so he could prove how virile he was.

She frowned. Virile? If she'd been asked for a word to describe Clive, it certainly wouldn't have been virile. That would have been like describing herself as sexy, and she would never in a million years describe herself as sexy.

When had she ever had wild sex with a man while still wearing all her clothes? No one had ever been that desperate for her, had they? Not even Clive. Certainly not Clive.

When Clive had come home from the office they'd talked about household accounts, mending the leaking tap, whether or not they should have his mother for the weekend. Never had he walked through the door and grabbed her, overwhelmed by lust. And she wouldn't have wanted him to, Jenna admitted to herself. If he had grabbed her she would have been thinking about all the jobs she still had to do before she could go to bed.

Blissfully unaware that her mother was thinking about sex, Lexi scuffed her trainer on the ground. 'There would have been loads for me to do in London. Cool stuff, not digging up bits of pot from muddy ground. I could have done my own thing.'

'There will be lots of things to do here.'

'On my own. Great.'

'You'll make friends, Lex.'

'What if I don't? What if everyone hates me?'

Seeing the insecurity in her daughter's eyes, Jenna hugged her, not confessing that she felt exactly the same way. Still, at least the people here wouldn't be gossiping about her disastrous marriage. 'They won't hate you. You make friends easily, and everyone on this island is friendly.' Please let them be friendly. 'That's why we're here.'

Lexi leaned on the rail and stared at the island mournfully. 'Change is the pits.'

'Change often feels difficult, but it can turn out to be exciting.' Jenna parroted the words, hoping she sounded more convincing than she felt. 'Life is full of possibilities.'

'Not stuck here, it isn't. Face it, Mum. It's crap.'

Ryan McKinley stood with his legs braced and his arms folded. His eyes stung from lack of sleep, he'd had no time to shave, and his mind was preoccupied by thoughts of the little girl with asthma he'd seen during the night. He dug his mobile out of his pocket and checked for missed calls and messages but for once there were none—which meant that the child was probably still sleeping peacefully. Which was what he would have been doing, given the choice.

As the ferry approached the quay, he slipped the phone back into his pocket, trying not to think of the extra hour he could have spent in bed.

Why had Evanna insisted that *he* be the one to meet the new practice nurse? If he hadn't known that the woman had a teenage daughter, he would have suspected Evanna of matchmaking. He'd even thought of mentioning his suspicions to Logan McNeil, his colleague and the senior partner in the Glenmore Medical Centre. If she was planning something, Logan would probably know, given that Evanna was his wife. Wife, mother, midwife and—Ryan sighed—friend. She was a loyal, caring friend.

In the two years he'd been living on the island she'd done everything she could to end his hermit-like existence. It had been Evanna who had dragged him into island life, and Evanna who had insisted that he help out when the second island doctor had left a year earlier.

He hadn't been planning to work, but the work had proved a distraction from his thoughts, as she'd guessed it would. And it was different enough from his old job to ensure that there were no difficult memories. Different had proved to be good. The shift in pace and pressure just what he'd needed. But, as grateful as he was to his colleague's wife for forcing him out of his life of self-imposed isolation, he refused to go along with her need to see him in a relationship.

There were some things that wouldn't change.

'Hi, Dr McKinley. You're up early—' A pretty girl strolled over to him, her hair swinging over her shoulders, her adoring gaze hopeful. 'Last night was fun, wasn't it?'

'It was a good night, Zoe.' Confronted with the realities of living as part of a small island community, Ryan chose his words carefully. This was the drawback of living and working in the same place, he mused. He was her doctor. He knew about her depression and the battle she'd had to get herself to this point. 'You looked as though you were enjoying yourself. It was good to see you out. I'm glad you're feeling better.'

He'd spent the evening trying to keep the girl at a safe distance without hurting her feelings in front of her friends. Aware that her emotions were fragile, he hadn't wanted to be the cause of any more damage—but he knew only too well how important it was to keep that distance.

'I wasn't drinking alcohol. You told me not to with those tablets.'

'Probably wise.'

'I—' She pushed her thumbs into the pockets of her jeans, slightly awkward. 'You know—if you ever wanted to go out some time—' She broke off and her face turned scarlet. 'I shouldn't have said that. Millions of girls want to go out with you, I know. Sorry. Why would someone like you pick a screwball like me?'

'You're not a screwball.' Ryan wondered why the most difficult conversations always happened at the most awkward times. The ferry was docking and he was doing a consultation on the quay, within earshot of a hundred disembarking passengers. And, as if that wasn't enough, she was trying to step over a line he never allowed a patient to cross. 'You're suffering from depression, Zoe, and that's an illness like any other.'

'Yes, I know. You made me see that.' Painfully awkward, she rubbed her toe on the hard concrete of the quay. 'You've been great, Dr McKinley. Really great. I feel better about everything, now. More able to cope, you know? And I just wondered if—'

Ryan cut her off before she went too far and said something that couldn't be unsaid. 'Apart from the fact I'm your doctor, and I'd be struck off if I said yes, I'm way too old for you.' Too old. Too cynical. 'But I'm pleased you feel like dating. That's good, Zoe. And, judging from the way the men of Glenmore were flocking around you last night, you're not short of admirers, so I think you should go for it. Pick someone you like and get yourself out there.'

Her wistful glance told him exactly who was top of her list, and she gazed at him for a moment before giving a short laugh. 'You're refusing me.'

'Yes.' Ryan spoke firmly, not wanting there to be any mistake. 'I am. But in the nicest possible way.'

Zoe was looking at him anxiously. 'I've embarrassed you—'

'I'm not embarrassed.' Ryan searched for the right thing to say, knowing that the correct response was crucial both for her self-esteem and their future relationship. 'We've talked a lot over the past two months, Zoe. You've trusted me with things you probably haven't told other people. It's not unusual for that type of confidence to make you feel a bit confused about your own feelings. If it would help, you can change doctors.'

'I'm not confused, Dr McKinley. And I don't want to change doctors. You've got such a way with words, and I've never known a man listen like you—I suppose that's why I—' She shrugged. 'Maybe I will date one of those guys.' She smiled up at him. 'That archaeologist who's hanging around this summer is pretty cool.'

'Interesting guy,' Ryan agreed, relieved that she didn't appear to be too heartbroken by his rejection.

'What about you, Dr McKinley? Why are you waiting for the ferry? Are you meeting a woman?'

'In a manner of speaking. Our new practice nurse is arriving today. Reinforcements.' And he had a favour to ask her. He just hoped that Jennifer Richards was a big-hearted woman.

'A new nurse?' There was a wistful note to Zoe's voice. 'Well, I know Nurse Evanna needs the help. So what's this new nurse like? Is she young?'

'She's coming with her teenage daughter.' Why had Evanna wanted him to meet her? That question played on his mind as he watched the ferry dock. It could have been an innocent request, but he also knew that his colleague was obsessed with matching people up. She wanted a happy ending.

Ryan felt the tension spread across his shoulders. He knew life didn't often offer up happy endings.

Zoe's face brightened. 'If she has a teenage daughter, she must be forty at least. Maybe even older.' She dismissed the competition. 'Well, the ferry is on time, so you're about to meet your nurse.'

Shaking the sleep out of his brain, Ryan watched as a patchwork of people flowed off the ferry. Businessmen in suits, families clutching bulging beach bags, toddlers in pushchairs. A slightly overweight, middle-aged woman puffed her way towards him carrying a suitcase.

He didn't know whether to be relieved that Evanna clearly hadn't been matchmaking or disappointed that their new practice nurse didn't look fit enough to work a hard day at the surgery. 'Jennifer?' He extended a hand. 'I'm Dr McKinley. Ryan McKinley. Welcome to Glenmore Island.'

The woman looked startled. 'Thank you, but I'm Caroline, not Jennifer. I'm just here for a week with my husband.' She glanced over her shoulder towards a sweating, balding man, who was struggling with a beach umbrella and an assortment of bags, one of which popped open, spilling the contents onto the quay.

'Oops. Let me help you—' A slim girl put down her own suitcase, stepped forward and deftly rescued the contents of the bag, her pink mouth curving into a friendly smile as she stuffed everything back inside and snapped the bag firmly shut.

Ryan's gaze lingered on that mouth for a full five seconds before shifting to her snaky dark curls. The clip at the back of her head suggested that at one time her hair had been fastened, but it had obviously made an escape bid during the ferry journey and was now tumbling unrestrained around her narrow shoulders. She was pale, and there were dark rings under her eyes—as if she hadn't had a decent sleep in months. As if life had closed its jaws and taken a bite out of her.

He recognised the look because for months he'd seen it in his own reflection when he'd looked in the mirror.

Or maybe he was imagining things. Plenty of people looked tired when they first arrived on the island. It took time to relax and unwind, but by the time they caught the ferry back to the mainland they had colour in their cheeks and the dark circles had gone.

Doubtless this girl had worked all winter in some grey, smog-filled city, saving up her holiday for a couple of bracing weeks on a remote Scottish island.

Eyeing the jumper looped around her shoulders, Ryan realised that she obviously knew that summer weather on Glenmore could be unpredictable.

He watched her for a full minute, surprised by the kindness she showed to a stranger. With no fuss, she helped rearrange his possessions into a manageable load, making small talk about the problems of packing for a holiday in a destination where the weather was unpredictable.

Having helped the couple, the girl stood for a moment, just breathing in the sea air, as if she hadn't stood still for ages while the man and his wife carted themselves and their luggage towards the two island taxis.

'The brochures promise you a welcome,' the woman panted, her voice carrying across the quay, 'but I didn't imagine that the island doctor would meet everyone personally. He even shook my hand! That *is* good service.'

A faint smile on his lips, Ryan watched them pile into a taxi. Then he stared at the ferry, resisting the temptation to take another look at the girl. He hoped the nurse and her daughter hadn't missed the boat.

A hand touched his arm. 'Did I hear you say that you're Dr McKinley?' The girl with the tumbling black hair was beside him, cases by her feet, her voice smoky soft and her eyes sharp and intelligent. 'I'm Jenna.'

Ryan looked into her eyes and thought of the sea. Shades of aquamarine, green and blue blended into a shade that was uniquely hers. He opened his mouth and closed it again—tried to look away and found that he couldn't. So he just carried on staring, and he saw something blossom in the depths of those eyes. Awareness. A connection. As if each recognised something in the other.

Something gripped him hard—something he hadn't felt in a long time.

Shocked by the chemistry, Ryan inhaled sharply and prepared himself to put up barriers, but she got there first.

Panic flickered across her face and she took a step backwards, clearly rejecting what had happened between them.

And that was fine with him, because he was rejecting it too.

He didn't even know why she'd introduced herself. Was every passenger going to shake his hand this morning?

Ryan knew he needed to say something casual and dismissive, but his eyes were fixed on the sweet lines of her profile and his tongue seemed to be stuck to the roof of his mouth.

She wasn't a girl, he realised. She was a woman. A young woman.

Mid-twenties?

And she looked bone tired—as if she was ready to collapse into a big comfortable bed and sleep for a month.

'Sorry. I must have misheard—' Flustered, she adjusted the bag that hung from her shoulder. 'I thought I heard you say that you're Dr McKinley.'

'I did.'

'Oh.' Her tone suggested that news was unwelcome. Then she stuck out her hand. 'Right, well, I'm Jennifer Richards. Jenna.' She left her hand hovering in the space between them for a moment, and then slowly withdrew it as he simply stared at her. 'What's wrong? Have I arrived on the wrong day? You look a bit…stunned to see me.'

Jennifer Richards? Stunned didn't begin to describe his reaction. Ryan cleared his throat and shook her hand, noticing that her fingers were slim and cool. 'Right day.' Wrong description. 'It's just that—my partner fed me false information. I was expecting a woman and her teenage daughter.' Someone about twenty years older. Someone who wasn't going to make his hormones surge.

'Ah—' She glanced towards the ferry, her smile tired. 'Well, I'm the woman, but the teenage daughter is still on the boat, I'm afraid. That's her, hanging over the side glaring at me. She's refusing to get off, and I'm still trying to decide how best to handle this particular situation without ruining my reputation before I even take my first clinic. I don't suppose you have any experience in handling moody teenagers, Dr McKinley?'

He cleared his throat. 'None.'

'Shame.' Her tone was a mixture of humour and weary acceptance. 'This is one of those occasions when I need to refer to my handbook on teenagers. Stupidly, I packed it at the bottom of the suitcase. Next time it's going in my handbag and if necessary I'll ditch my purse. I apologise for her lack of manners.' She flushed self-consciously and looked away. 'You're staring at me, Dr McKinley. You're thinking I should have better control over my child.'

Yes, he was staring. Of course he was staring.

All the men on Glenmore were going to be staring.

Ryan realised that she was waiting for him to say something. 'I'm thinking you can't possibly be old enough to be that girl's mother. Is she adopted?' Damn. That wasn't what he'd meant to say.

'No, she's all mine. I have sole responsibility for the behavioural problems. But it's refreshing to hear I don't look old enough. According to Lexi, I'm a dinosaur. And she's probably right. I certainly feel past it—particularly right now, when I'm going to have to get firm with her in public. Oh, joy.' The wind flipped a strand of hair across her face and she anchored it with her fingers. 'You're still staring, Dr McKinley. I'm sorry I'm not what you were expecting.'

So was he.

He wasn't ready to feel this. Wasn't sure he wanted to feel this.

Mistrusting his emotions, Ryan ran a hand over his neck, wondering what had happened to his powers of speech. 'You must have been a child bride. Either that or you have shares in Botox.'

'Child bride.' There was a wistful note to her voice, and something else that he couldn't decipher. And then she lifted her eyebrows as the girl flounced off the ferry. 'Well, that's a first. She's doing something I want her to do without a row. I wonder what made her co-operate. Lexi—' she lifted her voice slightly '—come and meet Dr McKinley.'

A slender, moody teenager stomped towards them.

Ryan, who had never had any trouble with numbers, couldn't work out how the girl in front of him could be this woman's daughter. 'Hi, there. Nice to meet you.'

Eyes exactly like her mother's stared back at him. 'Are you the one who gave my mum this job? You don't look like anything like a doctor.'

Ryan wanted to say that Jenna didn't look like the mother of a teenager, but he didn't. 'That's because I didn't have time to shave before I met the ferry.' He rubbed his fingers over his roughened jaw. 'I am a doctor. But I didn't give your mother the job—that was my colleague, Dr McNeil.'

'Well, whatever you do, don't put her in charge of family planning. As you can probably tell from looking at me, contraception is *so* not her specialist subject.'

'Lexi!' Jenna sounded mortified and the girl flushed.

'Sorry. It's just—oh, never mind. Being in this place is really doing my head in.' Close to tears, the teenager flipped her hair away from her face and stared across the quay. 'Is there an internet café or something? Any way of contacting the outside world? Or are we using Morse code and smoke signals? Or, better still, can we just go home, Mum?'

Ryan was still watching Jenna. He saw the pain in her eyes, the exasperation and the sheer grit and determination.

She looked like someone who was fighting her way through a storm, knowing that there was no shelter.

Interesting, he mused, that Glenmore so often provided a bolthole for the wounded.

He wondered what these two were escaping.

Sensing that Jenna was hideously embarrassed, he knew he ought to say something—but what did he know about handling teenagers? Nothing. And he knew even less about what to say to soften the blow of teenage rudeness. Assuming that something along the lines of *she'll be leaving home in another four years* wouldn't go down well, Ryan opted to keep his mouth shut.

He'd never raised a child, had he?

Never been given that option. Anger thudded through him and he stilled, acknowledging that the feelings hadn't gone away. He'd buried them, but they were still there.

Taking an audible breath, Jenna picked up their bags. 'We're renting a cottage at West Beach. Is there a bus that goes that way?'

'No bus. There are taxis, but before you think about that I have a favour to ask.'

'What favour can I possibly do you already?'

Ryan gently prised the suitcases from her cold fingers, sensing the vulnerability hidden beneath layers of poise and dignity. 'I know you're not supposed to officially start until tomorrow, but we're snowed under at the surgery. I'm supposed to exert my charm to persuade you to start early, only I was up three times in the night so I'm not feeling that charming. I'd appreciate it if you'd cut me some slack and say yes.'

'You do house-calls?'

'Is that surprising?'

'The doctors I worked with rarely did their own house-calls. It was the one thing—' She broke off and smiled at him, obviously deciding that she'd said too much.

'On Glenmore we can't delegate. We don't have an out-of-hours service or a local hospital—it's just the three of us.' He looked at her pointedly. 'Four now. You're one of the team.' And he still wasn't sure what he thought about that.

'Are you sure you still want me? You're sure you don't want to rethink my appointment after what Lexi just said?' Her tone was light, but there was vulnerability in her eyes that told him she was worrying about her daughter's comments.

Ryan was surprised that she was so sensitive to what others might be thinking. Out of the blue, his mind drifted to Connie. Connie hadn't given a damn what other people thought. She'd been so monumentally selfish and self-absorbed that it had driven him mad.

'Your qualifications are really impressive. We're delighted to have you here. And the sooner you can start the better.'

'I spoke to Evanna McNeil on the phone.' She turned her head and checked on her daughter. 'She's arranged for us to pick up the keys to the cottage this morning. I was going to spend the day settling in and start work tomorrow.'

'The cottage isn't far from here. And I know you were supposed to have today to settle in, but if there is any way I can persuade you to start work this morning that would be fantastic. There's a clinic starting at eight-thirty, and the girl who helps Evanna with the kids is off sick so she has to look after the children. I'd cancel it, but we're already overrun because we've been down a nurse for a few months.'

'But if the clinic starts at eight-thirty that's just half an hour from now.' Jenna glanced at her watch, flustered by his request, working out the implications. 'I want to help, of course. Normally I'd say yes instantly, but—well, I haven't made any arrangements for Lexi.'

'I'm not six, Mum. I'll stay on my own.' The girl looked round with a despairing look on her face. 'I'm hardly likely to get into danger here.'

Ryan had a feeling that the child would be capable of getting into trouble in an empty room, and Jenna was clearly of the same opinion because she looked doubtful.

'I'm not leaving you on your own until we've both settled in and found our feet. It's going to be OK, Lex.' Her gaze was fixed on her daughter's face and Ryan wanted to ask *what* was going to be OK. What had given her dark rings around her eyes? What was keeping her awake at night?

Why had she taken a job on a remote Scottish Island?

It didn't take a genius to sense that there was a great deal more going on than was revealed by their spoken communication. And he couldn't help noticing that no man had followed her off the ferry. If there was a Mr Richards, then he was keeping his distance.

With customary practicality, Ryan searched for a solution. 'Lexi can come too. The surgery is attached to the house. She can hang out with Evanna and the children. Evanna would be glad of the help, and it will give Lexi a chance to find out something about the island. And I can drive you over to the cottage at lunchtime. I'll even help you unpack to speed things up.'

'Mum!' Lexi spoke through gritted teeth. 'I'm not spending the morning looking after a couple of babies! I'd rather go to broken pottery camp, or whatever it's called!'

Ryan struggled to think like a teenager. 'Evanna has internet access, and the mobile signal is great from her house.'

Lexi gave a wide smile that transformed her face from sullen to stunning. 'Then what are we waiting for? Lead me to civilisation. Otherwise known as wireless broadband.'

CHAPTER TWO

'I NORMALLY see Nurse Evanna,' the old lady said, settling herself into the chair. 'She knows exactly what to do with my leg.'

Could today get any worse? Feeling mentally exhausted, Jenna scanned the notes on the screen.

Not only did her daughter not want her to be here, the patients didn't appear to want her either. And doubtless Dr McKinley was also regretting her appointment after that embarrassing scenario on the quay.

And to top it all, having not thought about sex for what seemed like the whole of her twenties, she'd looked into Ryan McKinley's cool blue eyes and suddenly started thinking about nothing but sex. She'd been so mesmerised by an alien flash of chemistry that she'd almost embarrassed herself.

Jenna cringed at the memory of just how long she'd stared at him. Who was she kidding? She *had* embarrassed herself. There was no almost about it.

And she'd embarrassed him.

Why else would he have been staring at her?

What must he have thought?

That she was a sad, desperate single mother who hadn't had sex for a lifetime.

He'd made all those polite noises about her looking too young to have a teenage daughter, but Jenna knew it was nonsense. People said that, didn't they? People said *You don't look thirty*, while secretly thinking you looked closer to forty. She shuddered, appalled at the thought that he might be sitting in his consulting room right now, formulating a strategy for keeping her at a distance. She needed to make sure he knew she didn't have designs on him—that a relationship with a man was right at the bottom of her wish list.

She was just trying to survive. Rebuild her life.

Knowing she couldn't afford to think about that now, Jenna concentrated on her patient. 'I understand that it's unsettling to have someone new, Mrs Parker, but Evanna has left detailed notes. If you see me doing anything differently, or anything that makes you feel worried, you can tell me.'

'You've a teenage daughter, I hear?' Mrs Parker dropped her bag onto the floor and slipped off her shoe. Her tights were the colour of stewed tea and twisted slightly around her ankles.

Jenna searched through the choice of dressings available to her, unsure what the surgery stocked. 'I only stepped off the ferry half an hour ago. Word travels fast.'

'Hard to have secrets on Glenmore. We're a close community.'

'That's why I chose to come here, Mrs Parker.' That and the fact she hadn't had much choice. She helped the woman onto the trolley. 'And I don't have any secrets.'

'Will your husband be joining you later?'

'I'm no longer married, Mrs Parker.' Jenna swiftly removed the old dressing, wondering why saying those words made her feel such a failure.

As if to reinforce those feelings, Mrs Parker pressed her lips together in disapproval. 'I was married for fifty-two years. In those days we sorted out our differences. We didn't give up.'

Great. Just what she needed. A lecture. Still, she was used to those from her mother. She'd grown up seeing her failings highlighted in neon lights.

'I admire you, Mrs Parker. I'm just going to check your blood pressure.'

Mrs Parker sniffed her disapproval. 'I'm here to have the dressing changed.'

'I know that. And I've already picked out what I'm going to use.' Reminding herself that building relationships was essential to the smooth running of the practice, Jenna was patient. 'But it's important to check your blood pressure every six months or so, and I can see from your notes that it hasn't been done for a while.'

'I don't see what my blood pressure has to do with the ulcer on my leg.'

'Sometimes ulcers can be caused by bad circulation rather than venous problems. I want to do an ankle blood pressure as well as taking it on your arm.'

Mrs Parker relaxed slightly. 'You obviously know what you're doing. All right. But I haven't got all day.'

Jenna checked her blood pressure, reminding herself that she'd always known this move wouldn't be easy. Not for her, nor Lexi.

'So you fell pregnant when you were still in school, by the looks of you.' Mrs Parker's lips pursed. 'Still, everyone makes mistakes.'

Jenna carefully recorded the blood pressure readings before she replied. 'I don't consider my daughter to be a mistake, Mrs Parker.'

There was a moment of silence and then the old lady gave a chuckle. 'Capable of standing up for yourself, are you? I like that. You're obviously a bright girl. Why have you moved all the way up here? You could be in some leading city practice. Or are you running away?'

Jenna sensed that whatever she told this woman would be all over the island by lunchtime, so she delivered an edited version of the truth. 'My marriage ended. I needed a change.

And this place has a good reputation. Logan McNeil has built a good practice.' She didn't add that she would have taken the job regardless, because it was as far from Clive and her parents as it was possible to get without leaving the country.

'Logan is a good doctor. So's Ryan McKinley, of course. But we all know he won't be around for long. He's a real high-flier. Used to work as one of those emergency doctors.'

Emergency doctor?

Confused, Jenna paused. 'How long has he lived here?'

'Came here two years ago and bought the old abandoned lighthouse that Ewan Kinaird had given up hope of selling. Too isolated for everyone. But not for Dr McKinley. Apparently isolation was what he wanted, and he paid a fair price for it. Didn't see him for most of that first year. Turned up occasionally in the village to buy supplies. Kept himself to himself. Never smiled. Some thought he was antisocial. Others thought he was recovering from some trauma or other. Certainly looked grim-faced whenever I glimpsed him.'

Jenna felt guilty for listening. Part of her wanted to cover her ears but she didn't want to be rude. And she was intrigued by Ryan McKinley. When she'd met him he hadn't seemed antisocial. Nor had he shown signs of trauma. He'd talked. Smiled. But she knew a smile often hid a secret. 'So how does he come to be working as a GP?'

'That was Evanna's doing. Won't let anyone be, that girl—especially not if they're in trouble. She coaxed him into helping out after the last locum left them in the lurch. She had baby Charlie, and Logan was managing the practice on his own. When he was needed, Ryan stepped up. But we all know he won't stick. He'll be off to some high-flying job before the tide has turned.' Mrs Parker took a closer look at her leg. 'What's your professional opinion of this, then?'

'I'm just taking a look now.' Jenna wondered what trauma had made a doctor qualified in emergency medicine buy a secluded lighthouse on an isolated island. 'How did you find out he was a doctor?'

'Oh, he kept it quiet.' Mrs Parker peered at her leg. 'But Fiona Grange crashed her car into a ditch in the middle of a storm and he happened to be passing when it happened. Some say he's the reason she's alive. Bones smashed, she was unconscious, and the air ambulance couldn't take off. And there was Dr McKinley, cool as a Glenmore winter, stopping the bleeding, extracting her from the car—shocked everyone, he did. Went from hermit to hero in the blink of an eye. But there was no hiding his profession after that. And he's been a good doctor, although he's private. Keeps himself to himself. Some think he's unfriendly. A bit cold.'

Unfriendly? Jenna thought about the man who had met her at the quay. He hadn't been unfriendly. Tired, definitely. Guarded, maybe. She would have described him as cool, but not cold.

'I'm going to take a proper look at your leg now.' Trying not to think about Ryan McKinley, Jenna washed her hands and opened the dressing pack. 'Your blood pressure is fine. How long have you had this problem, Mrs Parker?'

'I had it last summer and it went away. But then it came back.'

'Did you wear your compression stockings?' She glanced down at the tan stockings that had been placed neatly on the chair.

'Not as much as I'm supposed to.'

'They're not that comfortable, I know.' Jenna cleaned the wound and dressed it. 'That does look sore, you poor thing. Are you in a lot of pain?'

Mrs Parker relaxed slightly. 'I'm old. I'm always in pain. My bones ache every morning. The Glenmore winter is bitter. Like having your leg in the jaws of a shark.'

'I've only ever been here in the summer. My grandparents used to bring me. Tell me if this feels too tight.' Jenna bandaged the leg, applying most pressure to the ankle and gradually less towards the knee and thigh. 'Try and keep your leg up before you come and have that dressing changed next week. Have you tried putting a couple of pillows under your mattress? The aim is to let gravity pull the fluid and blood towards the heart. It will reduce the swelling. Can you move your ankle?'

'Yes. You've done a good job,' Mrs Parker said grudgingly. She stood up and put her stockings back on with Jenna's help. Then she reached for her bag. 'That dressing feels very comfortable, actually. But tell Evanna I'm sorry to have missed her.'

'I'll do that.'

Jenna watched as Mrs Parker walked slowly down the corridor, and then returned to the computer to type up the notes, sinking into the chair, exhausted. This was a huge mistake. She should have just bought a new flat in London, then she could have stayed in her job and Lexi could have stayed in her school.

Instead she'd chosen a small island where strangers were viewed with suspicion and where her life was going to be lived under a microscope.

She was an idiot.

Forcing herself to take several deep breaths, Jenna reminded herself that it was natural for the islanders to be wary of a new nurse. She just had to earn their trust.

Or maybe she should just buy another ferry ticket and get off this island as fast as possible. She sank her head into her hands, and then sat up quickly as she heard a rap on the door.

Ryan walked in. 'I owe you an apology. I had no idea Mrs Parker was your first patient. Talk about baptism of fire.'

Somewhere between meeting her on the quay and starting his surgery he'd shaved and changed. The faded jeans had been replaced by smart trousers and the comfortable tee shirt by a tailored shirt. In the confines of her consulting room he seemed taller. And broader. Suddenly she had no trouble imagining him as a high-powered consultant in a busy emergency department.

Her throat suddenly felt dry. 'Yes, she was my first patient.'

'You're still alive?'

Oh, yes. She knew she was alive because she could feel her heart banging hard against her chest. 'We did OK.'

'But now you want to resign?' His voice was dry. 'You're about to buy a return ferry ticket and run back to London?'

Jenna sat rigid, terrified that he'd guessed how bad she felt. 'No.' Her voice was bright. 'I'm not even remotely tempted to run away.'

His smile faded and his gaze sharpened. 'I was joking.'

'Oh.' She turned scarlet. 'Of course you were joking. Sorry. I'm a bit tired after the journey.'

'The last nurse we appointed lasted three days. Didn't Evanna tell you?'

'She did mention something. Don't worry, Dr McKinley. I'm not a quitter.' Jenna said it firmly, reminding herself of that fact. 'And Mrs Parker was fine.'

'I know Mrs Parker, so you must be lying.'

Yes, she was and it seemed that these days she spent her life lying. Even her smile was a lie. 'Mrs Parker was wary at seeing someone new, and that's normal—especially at her age. She doesn't like change. I understand that.' Jenna concentrated on the computer, thinking that she was finding change terrifying and she was several decades younger than Mrs Parker.

'That leg of hers is slow to heal.'

Jenna thought about the old lady—remembered how much had been said in a short time. 'I don't know her, but at a guess I'd say she doesn't really want it to heal. She's lonely. Her leg gives her a reason to come up here and interact with people.'

'That's possible.' His eyes narrowed thoughtfully. 'Despite your college-girl looks, you're obviously very sharp.'

Accustomed to thinking of herself as 'past it', his compliment made her feel strange. Or maybe it hadn't been a compliment. 'I'm interested in people. I like looking for the reasons they do things. It's why I do the job.' Even as she said the words she realised the flaw in that theory. If she was so interested in why people did what they did, why hadn't she spotted the signs that her husband was cheating on her? Maybe she wasn't so observant after all. Or maybe she hadn't wanted to see what was under her nose.

Feeling the tension erupt inside her, Jenna hit a button on the computer and exited Mrs Parker's file, wishing she could control her thinking. She had to stop asking 'what if?' She had to move on. That was what she was doing here, wasn't it? She was wiping out the past. 'Why do *you* do the job, Dr McKinley?' Would he tell her that he was an emergency specialist in hiding?

He was leaning against the wall, his broad shoulders threatening the safety of the asthma poster stuck to the wall. 'At the moment I can't remember. You'd better ask me that question again when I haven't been up for half the night doing calls. I'm always in a snarly mood when I get less than three hours' sleep.'

'That's understandable. Could you sneak off and sleep at some point today?'

'Unfortunately, no. Like I said to you on the quay—it's just the four of us. When we're busy, we're busy. We can't hand it over.'

'Who called you out last night? Locals or tourists?'

'One tourist with chest pains, a toddler with a febrile convulsion, and one of our own with a very nasty asthma attack.' He frowned. 'I called the mother a few moments ago to check on her and she told me the child is still asleep, but I'm going to call in later. I didn't like the look of her in the night. I gather you have an interest in asthma?'

'Yes. I ran a clinic in London.' Jenna was interested.

'Was there an obvious trigger? Did she have an infection or something?'

'They'd got themselves a dog from the rescue centre. I'm assuming it was that.'

'They didn't know that animal fur was a trigger?' Jenna pulled a face, understanding the ramifications of that state- ment. 'So is the dog being returned?'

'It's a strong possibility. They're thinking about it, but ob- viously the child will be upset.'

'It would be wonderful to have a dog,' Jenna said wistfully, and then sat up straight, slightly shocked by herself. A dog? Where had that thought come from? Why on earth would she want a dog?

'Maybe you could give this one a home?'

Jenna automatically shook her head. 'We can't have a dog. Cl—' She was about to say that Clive hated animals, but then she remembered that she wasn't married to Clive any more. His opinion didn't matter.

Glancing down at her left hand, she stared at the pale line on her finger that was the only remaining evidence that she'd once worn a ring. It still felt strange, seeing the finger bare. And it still brought a sting to the back of her throat.

'Something wrong?' His question made her jump.

'No. I was just thinking about your little asthma patient and the dog.'

'Right.' His gaze locked onto hers and she looked away quickly, thinking that Ryan McKinley was nothing like the men she usually met during her working day. For a start he was about two decades younger than the GPs she'd worked with in her last practice. She tried to imagine any of *them* ex- tracting a seriously injured girl from the wreck of a car during a storm without the help of paramedics—and failed. Ryan McKinley was a different breed of doctor. And then there was the fact that he was indecently good-looking. Sexy.

A different breed of man.

'You look really stressed out.' Ryan spoke quietly. 'Is that Mrs Parker's doing? Or is it being thrown in at the deep end?'

'No! Not at all.' Oh, God, he'd noticed that she was stressed. And the one thing she absolutely couldn't afford to do was put a foot wrong in this job. 'I love being thrown in at the deep end. Anyway, I didn't ask why you were here. Did you want to talk to me? Is there something I can help you with, Dr McKinley?' Please don't let him say he'd changed his mind about hiring her.

'I wondered if you could take some bloods for me.' Ryan handed her a form, his eyes still on her face. 'Callum is fifteen and he's showing all the signs of glandular fever. I know you already have a full clinic, but I really need these results as soon as possible.'

'Of course you do.' As she took the form from him, Jenna's fingers brushed against his. She immediately snatched her hand away, feeling as though she'd touched a live wire. 'I'll do them straight away.' Without thinking, she rubbed her fingers, wondering whether she was doomed to overreact around this man.

'He's in the waiting room with his mum.' Ryan was looking at her fingers, and Jenna swallowed and dropped her hands into her lap.

'Fine. Great. I'll call him.'

'I appreciate it.' There was a tension about him that hadn't been there before. 'Your bikes have been delivered, by the way. I had them taken straight to the cottage. They'll be safe enough outside your front door.'

'Bikes?' Jenna had to force herself to concentrate. 'Bikes. Yes, of course. Evanna told me about this place that hires them for the summer, so I rang them. I thought it would be good for both of us to cycle.'

'I'm impressed. It's a good example to set to the patients.'

'So you'll try not to knock me off my bike when you're accelerating past in your Porsche?'

He gave a faint smile as he strolled towards the door. 'Are you accusing me of speeding or being a couch potato?'

'Neither. I'm sure you're very fit.' Her eyes slid to the hard muscle of his shoulders, clearly outlined by the smooth fabric of his casual shirt. Damn, she shouldn't have used the word *fit*. Wasn't that the word Lexi used when she found a boy attractive? 'I mean, you're obviously athletic— I mean, health-conscious—sorry, just ignore me...' Jenna had the distinct impression that he was laughing at her, but when she looked at him his expression was unreadable.

'Why would I want to ignore you?'

'Because I'm talking nonsense—' And he was super-cool, hyper-intelligent and nothing like the men she usually dealt with. She had no trouble believing Mrs Parker's assertion that he was a top doctor. He had an air of authority and command that she found mildly intimidating. 'The bikes will be great.'

'Does Lexi know you've ordered bikes?'

'Not yet.' She didn't know which impressed her more, the fact that he'd remembered her daughter's name or his uncannily accurate assessment of her character. 'Light the touch paper and stand well back. Which reminds me; I owe you an apology for her behaviour earlier.'

'What do you have to apologise for?'

'Lexi. She—' Jenna didn't want to reveal personal details, but she was unable to bear the thought he might think badly of her daughter. 'She's very mixed up at the moment. She didn't want to move from our home in London. It's been hard on her.'

He was silent for a moment, considering her words. She had a nasty feeling that he knew just how close to the edge she was. 'Glenmore has a very calming effect on people. It's a good place to escape.'

'Lexi didn't want to leave London.'

'Perhaps your needs are greater than hers at the moment,'

he said gently. 'Does Lexi know you're living in a cottage on the beach?'

'No. There's only so much bad news that she can take at one time. She's going to hate me for not renting a house in the village.'

'That's not exactly a hub for entertainment, either.' He opened the door. 'When you've finished your clinic, knock on my door. I'll take you and your luggage over there.'

'I don't expect you to do that. If you have any spare time, you need to sleep.'

'I'll give you a lift.' He hesitated, his hand on the door. 'Give it a few weeks before you buy that ferry ticket. I predict that in no time this place will feel like home.'

He knew.

He knew how bad she felt. She'd done a lousy job at hiding her feelings. He knew she was panicking and having second thoughts.

Horrified that he was clearly aware of how close she was to breaking, Jenna just sat there, not trusting herself to speak. Their eyes held, and then he gave a brief nod.

'Welcome to Glenmore, Jenna. We're very pleased to have you here.'

Ryan stood in front of his colleague, legs spread, hands dug in his back pockets. 'Tell me about Jenna.'

'Jenna?' Logan McNeil signed a prescription and glanced up, his expression interested. 'Why? Was it love at first sight? Your eyes met across a crowded ferry ramp?'

Remembering the flash of chemistry, Ryan rolled his shoulders to ease the tension. 'Just give me the facts, Logan.'

Logan put his pen down. 'She's been working as a practice nurse in England for the past six years, but I'm not holding that against her. Why are you asking? Has she killed a patient or something?'

'I'm worried about her.'

'Isn't that a little premature? She's been here for five minutes.'

And he'd been worried about her within thirty seconds of meeting her. She'd looked fragile and battered, as though she'd emerged from a terrible storm. 'Evanna asked me to meet her, remember? She looks as though she's holding it together by a thread.'

Suddenly Logan wasn't smiling. 'You're worried about her ability to do the job?'

'No. She handled Mrs Parker, which proves she's more than capable of doing the job. I'm worried about *her*!' Ryan shot him an impatient look. 'What do you know about her personal circumstances?'

With a sigh, Logan opened his drawer and pulled out a file. Scanning the papers, he paused. 'Divorced with a teenage daughter. That's all it says.'

Divorced.

Ryan prowled to the window of Logan's consulting room and stared across the fields. Remembering the white circle on her ring finger, he was willing to bet the divorce was recent. Was that why she was so pale and drawn? Divorce did that to people, didn't it? Was that why she jumped when a man touched her? 'Was her ex-husband abusive?'

'I have absolutely no idea. This is her CV, not a police state-ment. Are you sure you're not going a little over the top here? You seem very concerned about someone you only met a few hours ago.'

Ryan turned. 'She's a colleague,' he said evenly. 'It's in our interest to make sure she's happy here.'

'And that's all that's going on here?' Logan closed the file. 'You seem very interested in her.'

'I didn't say I was interested. I said it was in our interest to make sure she's happy.'

'Good. Then I'll leave it to you to make sure she is.' Logan pushed the file back in the drawer. 'Plenty of people get divorced, Ryan. It's a fact of life in our society. It doesn't mean she has problems. You could be barking up the wrong tree. Has she seen the cottage yet?'

'I'm taking her at the end of morning surgery.'

'Let's just hope she likes isolation, otherwise we'll be looking for a new practice nurse. Ted Walker has a flat vacant in the village if you think that would be better.'

'I know she's going to like the cottage.' He didn't know how he knew, but he did.

She was running—wounded—looking for a place to hide and recover.

And the cottage was the perfect place for her. Whether her teenager daughter would survive the isolation was another matter.

CHAPTER THREE

IT WAS the prettiest house she'd ever seen—one of four fishermen's cottages facing the sea, their front gardens leading straight down to a sandy beach.

The iron gate was rusty and creaked as she pushed it open, but Jenna felt a sudden feeling of calm and contentment. No more endless traffic jams and road rage. No more rush hour. No more litter on the streets and graffiti on the walls.

Just open space, fresh air, and the sound of the sea.

It was perfect.

Lexi gave a whimper of horror. 'This is it? It's the smallest house I've ever seen.'

Jenna felt the tension return to her stomach. 'Small, yes, but it's ours.' As long as she kept the job. The house came with the job. They had a home again. And it would be cheap to run.

Lexi was gaping at the tiny cottage. 'A whole summer here?'

'Yes.'

'You can't swing a cat.'

'We don't have a cat.' But they might have a dog. She'd been thinking about it ever since Ryan McKinley had mentioned the idea.

Lexi closed her eyes. 'Just kill me now,' she muttered, and Jenna searched for something to say that would cheer her up.

'Don't you think this is better than London?'

'Tell me that isn't a serious question—'

Jenna sighed. They'd come this far. They had to keep moving forward.

She walked up the path to the front door, her eyes scanning the pretty garden. She noticed a few weeds and her hands itched. It would be fun, she mused, to have a proper garden.

Lexi stared desperately at the house and then at the beach. 'Where's the nearest shop?'

'Walk straight down the road and you reach the harbour. If it's low tide you can walk along the beach.' Ryan strode up the path behind them, carrying both suitcases. He deposited them on the ground, gently removed the key from Jenna's hand and opened the door of the cottage.

'Sorry—I was miles away.' Jenna gave a smile of apology. 'It's so long since I had a garden. Our house in London just had a courtyard. I'm not used to so much outdoor space.' Enchanted, she stooped and touched some of the pretty pink flowers that clustered by the door. *'Armeria maritima.'*

Ryan raised his eyebrows, apparently amused. 'You're quoting the Latin names of plants at me?'

'My mother was a botanist. I grew up hearing Latin names. Some of them stuck.' She touched the flower with the tip of her finger. 'Sea pinks. They grow well in this climate, by the coast.'

Lexi rolled her eyes. 'Gosh, Mum, gripping stuff.'

Jenna flushed and stood up. 'Sorry. It's just so wonderful to have a garden.' Despite the knot in her stomach she felt better, and she was in no hurry to go indoors. Instead she breathed in the sea air and watched the plants waving in the breeze. The grass needed cutting, and there were weeds in the borders, but somehow that just added to the charm. She imagined herself lying on a rug on a warm Sunday morning, listening to the gulls and reading the paper.

When had she ever done that? Sundays were normally so busy, what with making a traditional Sunday roast for Clive and his mother, and then being expected to produce tea for the cricket club...

Aware that Ryan was watching her, Jenna flushed. She felt as though he could read her every thought, and that was disturbing because some of the thoughts she'd been having about him were definitely best kept private. 'When Evanna told me that the job came with a house, I never imagined it would be anywhere as perfect as this. I can't imagine why anyone would want to leave here. Who owns it?'

'Kyla—Logan's sister. Her husband, Ethan, was offered a job in the States. They'll be back at some point.'

But not soon. Please don't let it be soon.

A warm feeling spread through her, and for the first time since she'd left London Jenna felt a flicker of hope. Excitement. As if this might be the right decision after all.

She felt as if she belonged. She felt at home.

It's—so peaceful.' A gull shrieked above her and she laughed as she caught Ryan's eye. 'Well, not peaceful, perhaps, but the noises are different. Good noises. No car horns and revving engines. And everything is slow. I'm looking forward to just being still.' Realising that she probably sounded ridiculous, Jenna shrugged awkwardly. 'In London everything moves so fast. You get swept along with it so that sometimes you can't even take a breath—I hate the pace of it.'

'That's because you're so old, Mum.' Lexi fiddled with her phone. 'London was exciting. And our house was lovely.'

'London was noisy and smelly and our house was far too big for the two of us.' It was what she'd told herself when she'd realised that their house had been sold and she and Lexi no longer had a home. It was the only way she had coped.

Pushing away that thought, Jenna stepped into the hallway of the cottage. They had a home now, and she loved it. Light reflected off the polished wooden floor, and through an open door she could see a bright, cheerful kitchen. 'We lived right next to an underground station and every three minutes the house shook.'

'Yeah, it was so cool.' Lexi tossed her hair away from her face, her eyes still on her mobile phone. 'I was never more than ten minutes from the shops.'

But Jenna wasn't thinking about shopping. It seemed far away. And so did Clive and the whole sordid mess she'd left behind. 'This place is wonderful. We can have our breakfast outside on that little table.' She turned to look at the pretty garden, eyes slightly misty, imagination running free. 'Lexi, you can go for a swim, or a run on the beach.'

How could this be a mistake?

Maybe she hadn't done the wrong thing. They could be happy here—she felt it.

Lexi shot her a look of incredulous disbelief and checked her mobile phone. 'No signal again. How do people function around here?'

'You can usually get a signal if you walk up the hill towards the castle.' Ryan lifted their suitcases into the hallway and Lexi gave an exaggerated sigh.

'Fine. If the only place I can use my phone is at the top of a hill then I'm going to have to walk up it!' Making a frustrated sound in her throat, she stalked away.

Jenna opened her mouth to say *be careful* and then closed it again, leaving the words unspoken. She knew from experience that too much maternal anxiety was counterproductive.

But the guilt was back, eating away at her like acid, corroding her insides. She might have fallen in love with the cottage, but she knew this wasn't what Lexi wanted.

'It must be hard, letting them grow up.' Ryan was standing in the doorway, his thumbs hooked into the pockets of his trousers, a speculative look in his blue eyes as he watched her.

'You have no idea.' Keeping her tone light, Jenna walked past him into the garden, her gaze on Lexi as her daughter sauntered across the road and started up the hill. A dozen nightmare scenarios sped through her overactive maternal brain. To control them, she used black humour. *Say it aloud and it might not happen.* 'Are there any scary, dangerous individuals at large on Glenmore at the moment?'

'Well, you've already met Mrs Parker—they don't come much scarier or more dangerous than her. She's wanted in five counties.' His arm brushed against hers and Jenna felt her whole body tingle.

She stepped away from him, keeping her distance as she would from an electric fence. 'I was thinking more of axe-wielding murderers and rapists.'

'We had dozens of those last summer, but Mrs Parker saw them off. It's hard to commit a crime in a community that knows what you're planning to eat for supper.'

As Lexi's figure grew smaller, and then vanished from sight, Jenna felt a moment of panic. Catching his eye, she gave an embarrassed laugh. 'Yes, I know—I'm overreacting. It's hard to forget this isn't London. You must think I'm crazy. *I* think I'm crazy!'

'That isn't what I'm thinking.'

'It would be if you knew what was going through my mind. It's taking all my will-power not to charge after her and follow her up that hill.'

His gaze shifted from her face to where Lexi had disappeared. 'I don't know much about teenagers, but at a guess I'd say that probably isn't the best idea.'

'Well, I'd have to be discreet, of course.' She made a joke of it. 'I'd probably start by sprinting up the hill and then drop to my stomach and crawl so that she couldn't see me.'

'You're going to have a hell of a job beating off an axe-wielding murderer if you're crawling on your stomach.'

'Never underestimate a mother protecting her young.'

'I'll remember that.' He had a deep voice. Deep and male,

with a slightly husky timbre that made her think things she hadn't thought for a long time.

Jenna breathed in slowly and stared at the ridge, trying not to think about his voice. 'I can't believe she made it up there so quickly. Lexi isn't really into exercise. It's amazing what the lure of a mobile phone signal can do to cure teenage lethargy. I hope she'll be OK.'

Ryan turned to her, and she noticed that the passing hours had darkened his jaw again. 'She's crossed the only road and she's still alive. She'll be fine. I'm not so sure about you.'

Her gaze met his and their eyes held.

The rhythm of her heart altered and the oxygen was sucked from the air. The world shrank to this one place—this one man.

Everything else was forgotten.

Mesmerised by those blue eyes, Jenna felt her body come to life, like the slow, sensual unfolding of a bud under the heat of the sun. Not the sultry, languid heat of summer sunshine but the fierce, rapacious scorch of sexual awareness. Like a volcano too long dormant after centuries of sleep, it exploded violently—blowing the lid on everything she believed herself to be. Excitement ripped through her like a consuming, ravenous fire, and in her newly sensitised state she found staring longingly at the firm lines of his mouth.

If she wanted to kiss him, she could…

She was a free woman now.

The shriek of a seagull brought her to her senses and Jenna took a step backwards.

What on earth was she thinking? If she did something crazy, like kissing him, he'd fire her from her job, Lexi would have a nervous breakdown, and she'd be more of an emotional wreck than she was already. And anyway, if she hadn't been able to trust someone she'd known for fifteen years, what chance was there with someone she'd known for fifteen minutes?

Jenna straightened her shoulders. 'You're right. I worry far too much about her. I intend to work on that this summer. I'm hoping it will be easier here.' Unfortunately her bright, businesslike tone did nothing to dissipate the strange turbulence inside her. She needed to be on her own, so that she could undo whatever she'd just done to herself by looking at him. And she was sure he was desperate to escape from her, albeit for different reasons.

'Thanks so much for the lift, Dr McKinley. I'm sorry to hold you up.'

'You're not holding me up.' Instead of leaving, as she'd expected, he walked back towards the house. 'Do you have any caffeine?'

Pulling herself together, Jenna followed him. 'Pardon?'

'Caffeine. I'm feeling tired, and there's still most of the day to get through.' Suppressing a yawn, he walked through to the kitchen without asking for directions or permission. 'I need coffee. Strong coffee.'

'I thought you'd need to dash off somewhere—lunch, house-calls…' She had thought he'd be anxious to escape from her—the desperate divorcee…

'We try not to do too much dashing on Glenmore.' Concentration on his face, he pulled open a cupboard and rummaged through the contents. 'It's bad for the heart. Which do you prefer? Tea or coffee?'

'Either. I mean—I haven't had time to shop.'

'The kitchen should be stocked.'

'Oh.' Jenna was about to ask who could possibly have stocked the kitchen when the phone rang. She jumped. 'Who on earth can that be?'

'Why don't you answer it and see? Phone's in the hall.'

Jenna found the phone, answered it, and immediately wished she hadn't because it was her mother. 'Hi, Mum.' Oh, no, she absolutely didn't want to have this conversation with

Ryan McKinley listening. Why, oh, why had she given her this number? 'No, everything is fine—' All her newfound tranquillity faded as her mother's cold disapproval trickled down the line like liquid nitrogen, freezing everything in its path. 'No, the doctors here don't care that I'm divorced.' She lowered her voice and turned away from the kitchen, hoping Ryan couldn't hear her above the hum of the kettle. 'No, the patients don't care, either—' She squeezed her eyes shut and tried not to think of Mrs Parker. 'And I'm not trying to ruin Lexi's life— it's kind of you to offer, but I don't think living with you would have been the best thing, Mum. I need to do this on my own— no, I'm not being stubborn—'

The conversation went the way it always went, with her mother stirring up every unpleasant emotion she could. Reminding herself to get caller ID, so that she could speak to her mother only when she was feeling really strong, Jenna gripped the phone. 'Yes, I know you're very disappointed with the way things have turned out—I'm not whispering—'

By the time the conversation ended her throat was clogged and her eyes stung. Whatever magic the cottage had created had been undone. The knot was back in her stomach.

All she wanted was moral support. Was that really too much to ask from a mother?

Knowing that she wasn't capable of going back into the kitchen without making a fool of herself, Jenna stood for a moment in the hallway, still holding the phone to her ear. It was only when it was gently removed from her hand that she realised Ryan was standing next to her.

He replaced the receiver in the cradle and curved his hand over her shoulder, his touch firm. 'Are you all right?'

Jenna nodded vigorously, not trusting herself to speak. But the feel of his hand sent a warm glow through her body. It had been so long since anyone had touched her. She'd been divorced for months, and even during her marriage there hadn't been that much touching. Clive had never been tactile. More often than not he'd had dinner with clients or colleagues, which had meant she was in bed and asleep long before him. Even when they had made it to bed at the same time he'd been perfunctory, fumbling, as if making love to her had been another task on his 'to do' list and not something to be prolonged.

She was willing to bet that Ryan McKinley had never fumbled in his life.

His broad shoulders were there, right next to her, and Jenna had a powerful urge to just lean against him for a moment and see if some of his strength could be transferred to her by touch alone.

They stepped back from each other at exactly the same time, as if each had come to the same conclusion.

Not this. Not now.

'I found the coffee.' His voice was rough. 'We need scissors or a knife to open this.'

Blinking rapidly to clear the tears misting her eyes, Jenna saw that he was holding a packet of fresh coffee in his free hand. 'Great.' Appalled to realise how close she'd come to making a fool of herself, she took the coffee from his hand and walked back into the kitchen. Keeping her back to him, she opened the drawers one by one until she found a knife.

He followed her. 'Does a conversation with your mother always upset you like this?'

'How do you know it was my mother?'

'I heard you say, "Hi, Mum".'

'Oh.' If he'd heard that, then he'd heard everything—which meant that there was no point in trying to keep the messy details of her life a secret. Jenna stared down at the knives in the drawer. 'Stupid, isn't it? I'm thirty-three. She shouldn't have an effect on me, but she does. She has a talent for tapping into my deep-seated fears—exposing thoughts I'm having but would never admit even to myself.' She closed her fingers around the handle of a knife. 'She thinks I've made the wrong decision, coming here.'

'And what do you think?'

'I don't know any more.' The tears were back in her eyes, blurring her vision. 'I thought I was doing the right thing. But now I'm worrying that what's right for me might be wrong for Lexi. I've uprooted her. I've dragged her away from everything familiar. We had to leave our home, but I didn't have to come this far away—' Taking the knife from the drawer, Jenna turned, wishing she hadn't said so much. 'Sorry. You wanted a cup of coffee, not a confessional. My call has held you up. If you want to change your mind and get on with your day, I quite understand.'

It was mortifying, having your life exposed in front of a stranger.

'I'm not leaving until I've had my coffee. I'm not safe to drive.' He leaned against the granite work surface, thumbs hooked in his pockets. 'Why did you have to move?'

'I'm divorced.' There seemed no point in not being honest. Why keep it a secret?

It had happened. There was no going back. She had to get used to it.

The problem was that once people knew you were divorced, they inevitably wanted to know why.

Jenna stared at the coffee in her hand, trying not to think about the girl with the long legs and the blond hair who had been lying on her husband's desk having crazy, abandoned sex. When had *she* ever had crazy, abandoned sex? When had *she* ever lost control? Been overwhelmed—?

'Careful! You're going to cut yourself—' A frown on his face, Ryan removed the knife from her hand. 'In fact you have cut yourself. Obviously this isn't a conversation to have while you're holding a sharp object. Let me look at that for you.'

Jenna watched as blood poured down her finger. 'Oh!'

Ryan took her hand and held it under the tap, cleaned it and then examined the cut. 'We need to find a plaster. Call me traditional, but I prefer milk in my coffee.' He was cool and calm, but Jenna was thoroughly embarrassed, and she tugged her hand away from his, dried it in a towel and applied pressure.

'Stupid of me. I don't know what I was thinking.'

'You were thinking of your ex-husband. Perhaps I should clear the knives out of the cutlery drawer.'

'You don't need to worry about me. I'm fine.'

'Obviously not, or your hand wouldn't be bleeding now. And no one emerges from divorce completely unscathed.'

'I didn't say I was unscathed, Dr McKinley. I said I was fine.'

'Ryan—' He handed her another piece of kitchen roll for her finger. 'Call me Ryan. Round here we tend to be pretty informal. Do you always pretend everything is OK when it isn't?'

'I'm just starting a new job. I don't want everyone knowing I have baggage.' She pressed her finger hard, trying to stop the bleeding, exasperated with herself. 'It won't affect my work.'

'No one is suggesting that it would. Everyone has baggage, Jenna. You don't have to wrap it up and hide it.'

'Yes, I do. For Lexi's sake. I've seen couples let rip at each other through their kids and there is no way I'm going to let that happen. I refused to let it be acrimonious. I refuse to be a bitter ex-wife.'

'So you grit your teeth and shed your tears in private?' Ryan took her hand and strapped a plaster to her finger.

'Something like that.' She'd bottled up the humiliation, the devastation, the sense of betrayal—the sense of failure. All those years people had been waiting for her to fail. And she'd failed in spectacular style.

Feeling the familiar sickness inside her, Jenna snatched her hand away from his. 'Sorry. I'm talking too much. If you're sure you still want it, I'll make you that coffee.'

'I'll make it. You press on that finger.'

Watching him perform that simple task with swift efficiency, Jenna couldn't help comparing him with Clive, who had never made her a cup of coffee in all the years they'd been together. 'Do you live far from the practice, Dr Mc— Ryan?'

'In the old lighthouse, three bays round from this one. You can walk there in twenty minutes along the coast path.'

Jenna remembered what Mrs Parker had said about him living like a hermit. 'The views must be fantastic. If I had a lighthouse, I'd have my bedroom right in the top so that I could look at the view.'

'Then we think alike.' He poured fresh coffee into two mugs. 'Because I have a three-hundred–and-sixty-degree view from my bedroom.'

For some reason Jenna had a vision of Ryan sprawled in bed, and she felt a strange flutter behind her ribs, like butterflies trying to escape from a net.

'Lucky you.' Her image of leaning against his shoulder for comfort morphed into something entirely different. Different and dangerous.

She stood up quickly. 'Why don't we drink this in the garden?' The fresh air would do her good, and the kitchen suddenly seemed far too small. Or maybe he seemed too big. Something was definitely out of proportion.

'Why did you have to leave your home?' He followed her outside and put the coffee down on the wooden table. 'Couldn't you have bought him out?'

'He sold the house.' She felt her hair lift in the breeze and breathed in deeply, smelling the sea. 'He put it on the market without even telling me. I was living there with Lexi, and then one morning I woke up to find three estate agents on my doorstep.'

'Did you get yourself a good lawyer?'

'Clive *is* a lawyer,' Jenna said wearily. 'And I didn't want

Lexi seeing her parents fighting. I wanted it to be as civilised as possible.'

'Civilised isn't sending round estate agents with no warning.'

'I know. But if I'd created a scene it would have been worse for Lexi. Apparently what he did was legal. I was only eighteen when we married—I didn't check whose name the house was in. I didn't check a lot of things.'

'Legal, maybe—decent, definitely not.' His tone was hard and there was a dangerous glint in his eyes. 'Does Lexi know he made you sell?'

'Yes. I told her the truth about that. I'm not sure if that was the right thing to do or not. She was already very angry with Clive for going off with another woman. And furious with me for choosing to relocate to Scotland.'

'Why *did* you choose Scotland?'

'Because it's a long way from London...' Jenna hesitated. 'Clive doesn't want Lexi around at the moment. He's living the single life and he sees her as a hindrance. I thought it would damage their relationship for ever if she found out he doesn't want her there, so I picked somewhere so far away it would be a logistical nightmare for her to spend time with him. I didn't want her having another reason to hate him.'

Ryan watched her for a long moment. 'No wonder you're exhausted. Lexi's a lucky girl, having a mother who cares as much as you do.'

'I don't know. Maybe I care too much. Maybe I'm protecting her too much. Or maybe I'm protecting myself. I don't want to admit that the man I was married to for fifteen years can behave like that. Anyway, this is a very boring for you.' Tormented by guilt, and depressed after the conversation with her mother, Jenna took a deep breath. 'Sorry. I'm lousy company, I know. Take no notice. I'm just tired after the journey. I'm sure you're really busy.'

'Why didn't your mother want you to come here?'

Jenna watched the sunlight spread across the pretty garden. 'She wanted us to move in with her. She said it would save money.'

'Save money, but not your sanity. I gather you resisted?'

'Yes. I thought we'd be better off having a fresh start, away from everyone. Clive has another woman. Actually, it turned out he had several women throughout our marriage…' Her face was scarlet. 'I was the last person to know. That's another reason I wanted to get away. That and the fact that the girl he's started seeing is twenty-two. It was really difficult for Lexi.'

'And you, I should imagine.'

She didn't even want to think about how she'd felt. 'The hardest thing was seeing Lexi so hurt. I thought if we moved here we'd be right away from it. I thought it would be good— but at the moment she just hates me for dragging her away from her friends. She's worried no one here will speak to her. And I have no idea why I'm telling you all this.'

'Because I asked. And don't worry about no one speaking to her. This is Glenmore,' Ryan said dryly. 'There aren't enough people here for anyone to be ignored. It's a small community.'

'I hope she doesn't get into any trouble.' Jenna stared over her shoulder towards the grassy hill where Lexi had disappeared. 'I think she's very vulnerable at the moment.'

'If it's any consolation, there are not a lot of places to find trouble here. Mrs Parker aside, the crime rate on Glenmore is very low. When we do have trouble it's almost always tourists and nothing serious. Nick Hillier, the island policeman, has a pretty boring job. If there's a group of tourists drunk on the beach then it's an exciting day for him. You have nothing to worry about.'

'I'm a mother. Worrying yourself to death is part of the package. It never changes. From the moment they're born, you're worrying. When they sleep you check them every five minutes to see if they're breathing. Once I even woke Lexi up in the night just to check she was alive. Can you believe that?'

His eyes amused, Ryan reached for his coffee. 'Our new mothers' group will love you. They talk about that sort of stuff all the time and I just nod sagely and say it's all normal.'

'But you're secretly thinking they're a bit odd?'

'Waking a sleeping baby? I have mothers tearing their hair out because the baby doesn't sleep, so, yes, it seems a bit odd to hear mothers worrying when the baby does sleep.'

'Once you have children you worry about everything, from sharp knives to global warming. And it doesn't stop.' Jenna shook her head, finding it a relief to talk to someone. He was a good listener. 'Will they fall off that bike they're riding? Will they remember to look both ways when they cross the road? You want them to be polite to people, and then you're worried they'll be too polite and might go off with some stranger because they don't want to give offence–'

'Jenna, relax! You're going to give yourself a nervous breakdown and you haven't even unpacked yet. You need to learn to chill.'

'Chill? What's that?' Jenna rolled her eyes in self-mockery. 'I don't know how to chill. But at work I'm sane, I promise. You must be wondering why on earth you gave me a lift. And a job.'

'Your job is safe. I can promise you that.'

'There's no such thing as safe.' She rubbed her finger over the table, following the grain of the wood. 'A year ago I had a husband, a home and a job. I lost all three.'

He was silent for a long moment. 'And now you have a home and a job again.'

There was something in his voice that made her look at him—made her wonder what personal trauma had driven him to this island.

'What I want is for Lexi to be happy.' Feeling calmer than she'd felt for ages, Jenna slipped off her shoes and curled her toes into the grass. 'I'm hoping that this will be a fresh start. I want it to feel like home.'

'If you need any help turning it into a home, give me a shout.' Ryan checked his watch and rose to his feet. 'I'm pretty good with a toolbox. Do you want any help unpacking? Is any of your furniture coming over?'

'No. No furniture.' Clive had claimed the furniture and all the belongings they'd collected over fifteen years of marriage. She hadn't had the strength to argue. She'd packed her clothes, a few books and not much else. 'I need to go shopping—oh, you said someone had stocked the place already?'

'When Evanna told the town meeting that you were coming, everyone from the village contributed.'

Jenna blinked. 'A group of people sat down and discussed my shopping list?'

'There's not a lot going on around here when the nightclubs are closed.'

'That's really kind.' Touched, Jenna made a mental note to thank everyone. 'Perhaps you could tell me the names. Then I can work out how much I owe everyone and pay them back.'

Ryan gave a faint smile, rolling up his shirtsleeves, revealing arms as strong as his shoulders. 'Oh, you'll pay. Don't worry about it. Everyone will claim a favour from you at some point. Usually at the most awkward, embarrassing moment, because that's how it works around here. One minute you're buying yourself a loaf of bread and the next you're giving an opinion on someone's rash.' He stood up. 'If we can do anything to help you settle in faster, let us know. The key to the back door is in the top drawer in the kitchen. It can be temperamental. If it jams, jiggle it slightly in the lock. And the shower turns cold if someone turns on a tap in the kitchen.'

'You know this house?'

'I stayed here for a few nights before I completed the sale on the lighthouse.'

'Oh.' Jenna had a disturbing image of him walking around the kitchen—showering in the bathroom. Naked.

Oh, God, she was losing it.

He raised an eyebrow. 'Are you all right?'

'Absolutely. How long should it take Lexi to get to the top and back? When do I start worrying?'

'You don't.' Ryan looked at the grassy ridge. 'She's on her way down now. I'll leave you to it. Surgery isn't until four. You can have a few hours to settle in. Spend some time together.'

'Yes.' Conscious that Lexi was approaching, Jenna lost her sense of calm. 'Thanks for the lift. And thanks for listening.'

He gave a brief nod and strolled out of her gate towards the sleek sports car that had transported her and her luggage from the surgery to the cottage. Without pausing in his stride, he exchanged a few words with Lexi as she sauntered past.

Watching anxiously from the garden, Jenna couldn't hear what he said, but whatever it was had Lexi smiling and that was an achievement in itself. Bracing herself for more complaints about her new home, she smiled at her daughter. 'Did you get a signal?'

'Yes, but everyone was out. Or maybe they're all still asleep after a night clubbing. Lucky them.' Lexi glanced over her shoulder as the sports car growled its way up the road away from them. 'What was he doing here, Mum?'

'He gave us a lift, remember?'

'An hour and a half ago.'

An hour and a half? Was that how much time had passed? Startled, Jenna glanced at her watch. 'Well—we were talking.'

'About what?' Lexi stared at her suspiciously and Jenna felt herself blush.

'About work,' she said firmly. 'I'm new to this practice, remember?'

'Oh. Right. I thought for one awful minute you—' She broke off and Jenna stared at her, heart thumping.

'What?'

'Nothing.' The girl gave a careless shrug, but Jenna knew exactly what she'd been thinking— *That her mother had been showing interest in a man.*

Jenna walked back into the cottage, feeling the burden of responsibility settle on her like a heavy weight. Whatever happened, she mustn't do anything to make her daughter feel more insecure than she already did.

'Dr McKinley was telling me that he lives in a lighthouse.'

'Dr McKinley is really hot.'

'Lexi! You're fifteen years old.' Appalled, Jenna cast a look at her daughter, but Lexi had her head in the fridge.

'Nearly sixteen. Old enough to know when a man is hot. Don't worry—I don't expect you to understand. You wouldn't know a good-looking man if you fell over him.' She pulled some cheese out of the fridge and then noticed the empty mugs on the kitchen table. Suddenly the tension was back. 'You invited him in for coffee?'

No, he'd invited himself in for coffee. 'He was up all night with patients.' Jenna adopted a casual tone. 'He was tired. It was the least I could do after he'd helped us.'

'Oh, Mum—' Lexi rolled her eyes, visibly cringing. 'Poor guy, being trapped by someone desperate divorcee. I suppose he was too polite to refuse.'

Wondering if Ryan saw her as old and desperate, Jenna picked up the empty mugs and washed them by hand. 'Of course he was being polite.' She didn't need her daughter to tell her that. 'I'm going to spend a few hours unpacking before I do the clinic this afternoon. Come and see your bedroom.'

They wandered upstairs and Lexi stared into the pretty bedroom. It had been decorated in keeping with the beach setting, with white New England furniture. A rug with bold blue and white stripes sat in the centre of the white floorboards. 'This is mine?'

'Yes. We can put your duvet cover on the bed and—'

'Sorting out the bed isn't going to make this my home.'

'Home is where family is,' Jenna said softly, 'and I'm here with you.' She felt a pang as she saw the vulnerability in Lexi's eyes.

'Well, that doesn't mean anything does it?' Her tone was flippant. 'I mean—Dad just walked out. What's stopping you doing the same?'

'I'm not going to walk out, Lexi. Not ever.' Jenna sank onto the edge of the bed, wanting to reassure her daughter. 'I know how difficult this has been for you—'

'No, you don't! You haven't got a clue—you have no idea how embarrassing it is that my Dad is having sex with a girl not much older than me!' Her voice rose. 'It's gross!'

Jenna resisted the temptation to agree. 'I told you—adults have relationships, Lexi.'

'*You* were in a relationship,' Lexi hissed. 'With each other. Marriage is supposed to be for ever—isn't that what you taught me?'

Jenna bit her lip. 'Ideally, yes.'

'So why didn't you try and fix it with Dad?'

'He didn't want to fix it. And—' Jenna thought about everything that had happened. *The way he'd treated her.* 'Not everything can be fixed.'

'Well, don't tell me you know how I feel, because you have no idea.' Lexi flounced out of the room and locked herself in the bathroom.

Jenna flopped onto the bed, feeling wrung-out and exhausted.

It was will-power that drove her downstairs to fetch the suitcases. Will-power that made her unpack methodically, finding homes for her pathetically small number of belongings. Unfortunately her will-power wasn't strong enough to stop her from thinking about Ryan McKinley.

It was only when she was hanging her clothes in her wardrobe that she realised that they'd spent an hour and a half together and he'd told her nothing about himself.

Nothing at all.

CHAPTER FOUR

JENNA leant her bike against the wall near the quay, waving to Jim the ferryman.

'Morning, Nurse Jenna. Finished your morning clinic?' A grey haired lady with a stick ambled past her on the pavement and Jenna smiled.

'Yes, all done, Mrs Hampton. How's the hip?'

'It's a miracle. I've had my first good night's sleep for four years. I was dreading the operation, if I'm honest—probably wouldn't have gone ahead with it if Dr McKinley hadn't encouraged me.'

'Nurse Jenna?' Someone touched her arm. 'Sorry to bother you—'

The impromptu conversations continued, so that by the time she'd walked along South Quay and up to the row of terraced houses that overlooked the water she was ten minutes late.

Ryan was already there and glancing at his watch, a brooding frown on his handsome face.

Jenna quickened her pace and arrived breathless, although whether that was from rushing the last few metres or from the sight of him, she wasn't sure. After two weeks working alongside him she knew that her body did strange things when Ryan was near. It didn't matter that they kept every exchange strictly professional. That didn't alter the chemistry. She hadn't said anything, and neither had he, but they both knew it was there.

Funny, Jenna mused, that she could even recognise chemistry when she'd been with one man all her life. 'I'm so sorry I'm late—I was waylaid.'

'You did a clinic on the quay?'

'How did you guess?' Laughing, Jenna removed the clip from her hair. Smoothing her hands over her curls, she twisted it into a thick rope and secured it firmly. 'There was a strong wind on the coast road. I must look as though I've been dragged through a hedge backwards.'

His eyes moved from her face to her hair. 'That isn't how you look.'

Colour stung her cheeks and she felt a shaft of awareness pierce low in her pelvis. 'Did you know Abby Brown is pregnant? I saw her eating a double chocolate fudge sundae in Meg's Café to celebrate.'

Ryan gave a wry smile. 'Let's hope she doesn't keep that up throughout the pregnancy. Are you ready?' But before he could press the doorbell the door opened and a woman stood there, a baby in her arms and a harassed look on her face. 'Hello, Elaine.'

'Oh, Dr McKinley—come on in.' The woman stood to one side and almost tripped over the dog which was bouncing in the hallway. As his tail hit the umbrella stand flying, the woman winced. 'Whatever possessed me to say yes to a dog? Not only does he make Hope's asthma worse, he knocks everything over.'

'He's beautiful.' Jenna bent down and made a fuss of the dog, and the animal leaped up and tried to lick her face, sensing an ally.

'Sorry—we've failed to teach him any manners.'

'I don't mind.' Giggling, Jenna pushed the dog down. 'What's his name?'

'We haven't decided—at the moment he's just called Black.'
Jenna tried to look stern. 'Sit!'

Black sat, and Ryan lifted an eyebrow. 'That's the first time I've seen that animal do as it's told.'

Elaine was astonished. 'You're so good with dogs! Do you have your own?'

'No.' Jenna stared at the black Labrador, who stared back, tongue lolling, tail wagging over the floor. It was a long time since anyone had looked at her with such adoration and unquestioning trust. 'I don't have a dog of my own.'

A family, she thought, didn't have to be a mother, a father and two children.

'You should think about getting one—you're obviously good with animals.' Elaine ushered them into the living room. 'Hope's on the sofa. She's had a much better night. We kept Black locked in the garden shed, and I vacuumed all the dog hairs this morning, but I haven't quite got my head round taking him back to the home.'

Jenna followed Ryan into the sitting room and noticed that the little girl's face brightened when she saw him.

'Dr Mac—I've been eating ice cream and jelly.'

'For breakfast?' Ryan pulled a face and sat down next to the child. He admired her doll, had a solemn conversation about which outfit she ought to wear for the day, and then pulled out his stethoscope. 'Can I listen to your chest?'

'It's all better.'

'So I hear. That's good. Can I listen?'

'OK.' With a wide smile, the little girl lay back on the sofa and waited.

His hands infinitely gentle, Ryan listened to her breathing, and watching him with the child made Jenna's breath catch. He focused entirely on the little girl, listening to every word she said as if she were the most important person in the room. 'I've been thinking about the attack she had, Elaine.' He folded the stethoscope and slid it back into his bag. 'You say she's using a normal inhaler, is that right?'

'Yes.'

'I think that might be the problem. I want to try her with a spacer—it's a device that relies less on technique, which is very useful for younger children. It makes sure they inhale the complete dose. To see you're taught to use it properly I've brought Nurse Jenna along with me.' Ryan gave a self-deprecating smile. 'I'm the first to admit that training children in inhaler technique probably isn't my forte, so I've called in the experts. Jenna used to do it all the time in her last job.'

Jenna removed the spacer from her bag and showed Hope's mother how it worked, explaining exactly what she had to do. 'It's really that simple.'

'She's due a dose now,' Elaine said. 'Could you check we do it right?'

Jenna watched, made a few suggestions, and explained to Hope exactly why it was important for her to take the drug.

'I breathe in that space thing every time?'

'Every time.'

'If I do that can I keep Black?'

Elaine sighed. 'No, sweetie. Black has to go.'

Hope's eyes filled with tears. 'But I love him. I can't send him back to that horrid place. I made him a promise. I promised him he had a home now.'

Feeling tears in her own eyes, Jenna blinked rapidly, feeling every bit of Elaine's anguish as a mother.

Elaine sank onto the sofa and shook her head. 'I have to take him back, Hope.' Her voice cracked. 'We can't keep him here. I can't risk going through what I went through the other night with you. I know it's hard, but we have no choice.'

'But I promised him he'd have a home and be loved.' Hope was sobbing now, great tearing sobs that shook her tiny body.

'I promised him, Mummy, and I can't break a promise. He'll be all on his own again. He'll think no one loves him.'

'I'll have him.' Jenna blurted the words past the lump in her throat and then stood in stunned silence, absorbing two things. Firstly, that she'd just got herself a dog, and secondly that making that decision had felt incredibly liberating.

For once she'd thought about herself. Not Clive. Not her mother. Herself.

Realising that everyone was looking at her, she shrugged. 'I'd like to have him. Really.' She looked at Hope. 'And I'll love him and give him a good home. So you won't have broken your promise...'

A tearful Elaine exchanged glances with Ryan. 'You want to take the dog?'

'I do.' Jenna spoke the words firmly, almost defiantly. Like a wedding ceremony, she thought with wry humour. *Do you take this dog...?* Only she knew without a flicker of doubt that the dog would never disappoint her. 'I really do. My daughter will be thrilled. And any time you want to come and see him, or meet up on the beach to throw a stick or two, you just bang on my front door...'

Ryan took a deep breath. 'Jenna, perhaps you should think about this—'

'I've thought about it for about thirty years. I've wanted a dog since I was a child.'

But her mother had said no. Then Clive had said no.

The advantage of being her own woman, in charge of her own life, was that there was no one to say no. And even if someone did say no, she wasn't sure she'd listen any more. She'd been weak, she realised. She'd allowed her own needs to come second. Her life had been about what Clive wanted. What Clive needed. And she'd been so busy keeping him happy, determined to keep her marriage alive and prove her mother wrong, that she'd stopped asking herself what she wanted.

Jenna straightened her shoulders and stood a little taller. 'If you wouldn't mind holding on to Black for one more day. I need to buy a book, check on the internet—make sure I know what I'm doing. A patient I saw last week breeds Labradors—I'd like to give her a ring and chat to her before I take Black.' Suddenly she felt strong, and the feeling was good—almost as if happiness was pouring through her veins.

Elaine gave a delighted laugh, relief lighting her face. 'If you're sure?'

'I'm completely sure.' And she had no need to ask Lexi what she thought. Lexi had wanted a dog all her life. 'I can take him with me on my visits—tie him to my bicycle while I go indoors. When I'm in clinic he can either play with Evanna's dog, or just stay in our garden. I'll find someone to build a fence.'

Elaine looked worried. 'Black rarely does what people want him to do.'

'That's fine by me.' Jenna stroked her hand over the dog's head, thinking of how often she'd disappointed her own mother. 'Maybe he and I have something in common. Welcome to rebellion.'

'That would be a good name,' Elaine laughed. 'Rebel. You should call him Rebel.'

'Just hope he doesn't live up to his name,' Ryan said dryly, closing his bag. 'There's a dog-training session every Thursday night in the church hall. You might want to book him in.'

'He ate your favourite shoes?' Laughing, Evanna leaned across the table and helped herself to more lasagne. 'You must have been mad.'

'With myself, for leaving them out.' Jenna was smiling too, and Ryan found it impossible not to watch her because the smile lit her face. He loved the dimple that appeared at the corner of her mouth, and the way her eyes shone when she was amused.

She was smiling regularly now, and the black circles had gone from under her eyes.

Extraordinary, he thought, how Glenmore could change people. 'What does Lexi think of him?'

'She adores him. She's the only teenager on Glenmore up at dawn during the summer holidays, and that's because she can't wait to walk him.'

Evanna cleared her plate and looked longingly at the food. 'Why am I so hungry? Do you think I could be pregnant again, Logan?'

It was only because he was looking at Jenna that Ryan saw her smile dim for a fraction of a second. Then she pulled herself together and joined in the conversation, her expression warm and excited.

'Do you think you could be? Charlie is two, isn't he? What a lovely age gap.'

Evanna agreed. 'I always wanted at least four kids.'

Ryan wondered if he was the only one who had noticed that Jenna had put her fork down quietly and was no longer eating.

Perhaps it was just that she found the whole happy family scene playing out in front of her emotionally painful. Or perhaps it was something else.

She'd been happy enough until Evanna had mentioned having more children.

Evanna lost the battle with her will-power and helped herself to more food. 'Weren't you tempted to have more children, Jenna?'

Sensing Jenna's tension, Ryan shifted the focus of the conversation away from her. 'If you're planning more children, you're going to have to build an extension on this house, Logan.'

'They can share a room,' Evanna said. 'If it's a girl, she can share with my Kirsty. If it's a boy, with Charlie.'

She and Logan spun plans while Jenna relocated her food from one side of her plate to the other.

It was the question about children that had chased away her appetite, Ryan thought grimly, reaching for his wine. And now he found himself wondering the same as Evanna. Why hadn't she had more children? She clearly loved being a mother.

Evanna heaped seconds onto everyone's plate except Jenna's. 'Aren't you enjoying it, Jenna?'

Jenna looked up and met Ryan's gaze.

They stared at each other for a moment, and then she gave a faltering smile and picked up her fork. 'It's delicious.' With a determined effort she ate, but Ryan knew she was doing it not because she was hungry, but because she didn't want to hurt Evanna's feelings. She was that sort of person, wasn't she? She thought about other people. Usually to the exclusion of her own needs.

He'd never actually met anyone as unselfish as her.

He felt something punch deep in his gut.

'Ryan—you have to fill those legs and wide shoulders with something.' Evanna pushed the dish towards Ryan but he held up a hand.

'Preferably not adipose tissue. I couldn't eat another thing, but it was delicious, thanks. I ought to be on my way.' Sitting here watching Jenna was doing nothing for his equilibrium.

Why had he accepted Evanna's invitation to dinner?

Over the past weeks he'd made sure he'd avoided being in a social situation with Jenna, and he had a feeling she'd been doing the same. And yet both of them had said yes to Evanna's impromptu invitation to join them for a casual supper.

'You can't go yet.' Evanna's eyes flickered to Jenna. 'Finish telling us about dog-training.'

It occurred to Ryan that the supper invitation probably hadn't been impromptu. Watching Evanna draw the two of them together, he had a sense that she'd planned the evening very carefully.

'The dog-training is a failure.' Jenna finished her wine. 'I really ought to go. Lexi was invited out to a friend's house, and she's taken Rebel, but she'll be back soon. I want to be there when they drop her home. I don't like her coming back to an empty house.'

Ryan poured himself a glass of water. 'I saw her eating fish and chips on the quay with the Harrington twins last week. She's obviously made friends.'

'Yes.' This time Jenna's smile wasn't forced. 'People have been very welcoming. There's hardly an evening when she's in.'

Which must mean that Jenna was often alone.

Ryan frowned, wondering how she spent her evenings.

Was she lonely?

He realised suddenly just how hard this move must have been for Jenna. Her relationship with her mother was clearly strained and her husband had left her. She'd moved to an area of the country where she knew no one, taken a new job and started a new life. And her only support was a teenager who seemed to blame her for everything that had gone wrong. And yet she carried on with quiet dignity and determination.

Unsettled by just how much he admired her, he stood up. 'I need to get back. I have things to do.'

Like reminding himself that the worst thing you could do after a relationship went wrong was dive into another relationship. That was the last thing Jenna needed right now. As for him—he had no idea what he needed.

'You can't possibly leave now! I made dessert—' Evanna glanced between him and Jenna and then cast a frantic look at Logan, who appeared oblivious to his wife's efforts to keep the two of them at her table.

'If Ryan has things to do, he has things to do.'

'Well, obviously, but—I was hoping he'd give Jenna a lift.'

'I'll give Jenna a lift if she wants one,' Logan said, and Evanna glared at her husband.

'No! You can't do it, you have that—thing—you know…'

she waved a hand vaguely '…to fix for me. It needs doing—urgently.'

'Thing?' Logan looked confused, and Ryan gave a half-smile and strolled to the door, scooping up his jacket on the way. If Evanna had hoped for help in her matchmaking attempts then she was going to be disappointed.

'I don't need a lift,' Jenna said quickly. 'I brought my bike. I'll cycle.'

She was keeping her distance, just as he was. Which suited him.

Unfortunately it didn't suit Evanna.

'You can't cycle! It's late. You could be mugged, or you might fall into a ditch.'

'It isn't that late, and if I don't cycle I won't be able to get to work tomorrow. My bike won't fit into Ryan's car.' Ever practical, Jenna stood up. 'I hadn't realised how late it was. Supper was delicious, Evanna. Are you sure I can't wash up?'

'No—the dishwasher does that bit…' Evanna looked crest-fallen, but Jenna appeared not to notice as she dropped to her knees to hand a toy to Charlie, the couple's two-year-old son.

Catching the wistful look on her face, Ryan felt something tug inside him. He found her kindness as appealing as the length of her legs and the curve of her lips.

As she walked past him to the door he caught her eye and she blushed slightly, said another thank-you to Evanna and Logan and walked out of the house, leaving the scent of her hair trailing over his senses.

By the time Ryan had said his farewells and followed her out of the house Jenna was fiddling with her bike, head down. Something about the conversation had upset her, he knew that. He also knew that if he delved into the reason he'd probably upset her more. He strolled across to her, his feet crunching on the gravel. 'Are you sure you don't want a lift home?'

'Positive. I'll be fine, but thanks.' She hooked her bag over the handlebars and Ryan noticed that her movements were always graceful, fluid. Like a dancer.

'Mrs Parker was singing your praises this week.'

'That's good to hear.' Smiling, she pushed a cycle helmet onto her head and settled onto the bike. 'Under that fierce exterior she's a sweet lady. Interesting past. Did you know she drove an ambulance during the war?'

'No. Did she tell you that during one of your afternoon tea sessions?'

'She told you about that?' Jenna fastened the chin strap. 'I call in sometimes, on my way home. I pass her front door.'

And he had a feeling she would have called in even if it hadn't been on her way home. The fact that she had time for everyone hadn't gone unnoticed among the islanders. 'Her leg is looking better than it has for ages. I suspect it's because you're nagging her to wear her stockings.'

'It isn't easy when the weather is warm. She needs a little encouragement.'

'So you've been stopping by several times a week, encouraging her?'

'I like her.'

They were making conversation, but he knew she was as aware of him as he was of her.

Looking at her rose-pink mouth, he wondered if she'd had a relationship since her husband.

'Evanna upset you this evening.'

Her gaze flew to his. Guarded. 'Not at all. I was a little tired, that's all. Rebel sometimes wakes me up at night, walking round the kitchen. I'm a light sleeper.'

Ryan didn't push it. 'I walk on the beach most mornings. If you want help with the dog-training, you could join me.'

'I'll remember that. Thanks.' She dipped her head so that her face was in shadow, her expression unreadable. 'I'll see you tomorrow, Ryan.'

He was a breath away from stopping her. A heartbeat away from doing something about the chemistry they were both so carefully ignoring.

What would she do if he knocked her off her bike and tumbled her into the heather that bordered Evanna's garden?

'Goodnight.' He spoke the word firmly and then watched as she cycled away, the bike wobbling slightly as she found her balance.

He was still watching as she vanished over the brow of the hill into the dusk.

CHAPTER FIVE

'Two salmon fillets, please.' Jenna stood in the fishmonger's, trying to remember a time when she'd bought food that wasn't shrink-wrapped and stamped with a date. And she'd never bought fish. Clive had hated fish.

Was that why she now ate fish three times a week?

Was she being contrary?

Eyeing the alternatives spread out in front of her, she gave a faint shrug. So what if she was? The advantage of being single was that you could live life the way you wanted to live it.

She had a dog and a garden, and now she was eating fish.

'Just you and the bairn eating tonight, then?' Hamish selected two plump fillets, wrapped the fish and dropped it into a bag.

'That's right.' How did anyone have a secret life on Glenmore? After only a month on the island, everyone knew who she was. And what she ate. And who she ate it with. Strangely enough, she didn't mind.

'How was your dinner with Dr McKinley?'

All right, maybe she minded.

Wondering if the entire island was involved in the match-making attempt, Jenna struggled for an answer. 'Dinner was casual. With Evanna and Logan. Just supper—nothing personal.' She cringed, knowing she sounded as though she had something to hide. 'How's Alice doing?' Changing the subject quickly, she tried to look relaxed.

'Still rushing around. I say to her, "Rest, for goodness' sake." But does she listen?' Hamish added a bunch of fresh parsley to the bag. 'No, she doesn't. That's women for you. Stubborn. Alice would die if it meant proving a point.'

'Well, I saw her in clinic yesterday and the wound was healing nicely, so I'm sure she isn't going to die any time soon.' Jenna dug her purse out of her bag. 'How much do I owe you?'

'Nothing.' His weathered brow crinkled into a frown as he handed over the bag. 'As if I'd take money after what you did for my Alice. I said to her, "It's a good job you fell outside Nurse Jenna's house, otherwise it would have been a different story." You sorted her out, fed her, had a lovely chat.' He glanced up as the door opened behind her and a bell rang. 'Morning, Dr McKinley. Surf's up for you today. They had the lifeboat out this morning—two kids in trouble on the rocks round at the Devil's Jaws. Place is roped off, but they climbed over.'

Jenna froze. He was behind her? She'd thought about him all night—thought about the way he'd watched her across the table. He'd made her so nervous she hadn't been able to eat. And he'd noticed that she wasn't eating.

Adopting her most casual expression, she turned and looked.

He was standing in the doorway, a sleek black wetsuit moulding itself to every muscular dip and curve of his powerful shoulders.

The bag of salmon slipped from her fingers and landed with a plop on the tiled floor.

Hamish cleared his throat pointedly and Jenna stooped to retrieve her bag, her face as red as a bonfire. 'Good morning, Dr McKinley.' She turned back to the fish counter and developed a sudden interest in the dressed crab that Hamish had on display as she tried to compose herself. Over the past few weeks she'd had plenty of practice. In fact she was proud of how controlled she was around him.

They worked together every day, but so far she'd managed not to repeat any of the embarrassing sins she'd committed on her first day, like staring at his mouth. Even during dinner last night she'd managed to barely look at him.

And if she occasionally thought about how his hands had felt on her shoulders that day in her kitchen—well, that was her secret. A girl could dream, and she knew better than anyone that there was a world of difference between dreams and reality.

Jenna continued to stare at the crab. It was a shock to discover that, having thought she'd never trust a man again, she could actually find one attractive. But even if she could trust a man, the one thing she couldn't trust was her feelings. She knew she was hurt. She knew she was angry. And she knew that she was lonely for adult company.

This would be a bad, bad time to have a relationship even if one was on offer. Which it clearly wasn't—because, as Lexi was always telling her, she was past it. Why would Ryan want a relationship with someone like her?

'Thought I'd save you a journey and drop off that prescription.' Ryan handed it to Hamish. 'Did you know that crab personally, Jenna? You've been staring at him for the past five minutes.'

Jenna looked up, her inappropriate thoughts bringing the colour rushing to her cheeks. 'He has the same complexion as my first cousin.'

The corners of his mouth flickered. 'Yes? I can recommend a cream for that condition.'

She felt the breath catch in her throat because his smile was so sexy, and there was that unmistakable flash of chemistry that always occurred when they were together.

Imagining what it would be like to kiss a man like him, Jenna stared at him for a moment and then turned back to the crab, telling herself that even if things had been different she'd never have been sophisticated enough to hold a man like him. Ryan McKinley might be working on Glenmore, but she recognised a high-flier when she saw one. He was like one of those remote, intimidating consultants who strode the corridors of the hospital where she'd trained. Out of her league.

Hamish exchanged a look with Ryan and raised his eyebrows. 'You want to take a closer look at that crab?'

'No.' Flustered, Jenna pushed her hair out of her eyes. 'No, thanks— I— But it does look delicious.' Oh, for goodness' sake. What was the matter with her? Lexi was right—she was desperate. And she needed to leave this shop before she dropped her salmon a second time. Smiling at Hamish, she walked towards the door.

'Wait a minute, Nurse Jenna.' Hamish called after her. 'Has Dr McKinley asked you to the beach barbecue? Because if he hasn't, he's certainly been meaning to.'

Did everyone on Glenmore interfere with everyone else's lives?

Jenna looked at Ryan, who looked straight back at her, his expression unreadable.

Realising that Hamish had put them both in an impossible position, Jenna was about to formulate a response when Ryan straightened.

'It's on Saturday. In aid of the lifeboat. You should come.'

Knowing he'd only invited her because Hamish had pushed him, Jenna shook her head. 'I'm busy on Saturday.'

Hamish tutted. 'How can you be busy? Everything shuts early. Everyone on the island will be there. There's nothing else to do. Young thing like you needs a night out. You've done nothing but work since the day you stepped off that ferry.'

A night out?

When she finally felt ready for a night out it wouldn't be with a man like Ryan McKinley. When and if she did date a man again, she'd date someone safe and ordinary. Someone who didn't make her tongue knot and her insides turn to jelly. And preferably someone who didn't put her off her food.

He was watching her now, with that steady gaze that unsettled her so much. 'The islanders hold it every year, to raise funds for the lifeboat and the air ambulance. You're supposed to bring a dish that will feed four people. And wear a swimming costume.'

'Well, that's the end of that, then.' Somehow she kept it light. 'I can bring a dish to feed four people, but I don't own a swimming costume.'

'Swim naked,' Hamish said. 'Been done before.'

'And the culprits spent the night sobering up in one of Nick's four-star cells,' Ryan drawled, a sardonic gleam in his eyes. 'It's a family event. You can buy a costume from the Beach Hut, four doors down from here.'

Jenna had been into the Beach Hut twice, to buy clothes for Lexi. She hadn't bought anything for herself. 'Well—I'll think about it, thanks.'

Hamish scowled. 'You *have* to go. Isn't that right, Dr McKinley?'

Ryan was silent for a moment. 'I think Jenna will make her own decision about that.'

Jenna flushed. He wasn't going to coerce her. He wasn't going to tell her whether she should, or shouldn't go. He was leaving the choice up to her.

And that was what she did now, wasn't it? She made her own choices.

She decided whether she owned a dog and whether she was going to eat fish.

She shivered slightly, barely aware of the other customers who had entered the shop. She was only aware of Ryan, and the multitude of confusing feelings inside her. If she had to make a decision, what would it be?

She wanted to ask him whether he wanted her to go. She wanted to apologise for the fact that the islanders were match-making. She wanted him to know it had nothing to do with her.

Hideously embarrassed, she muttered that she'd think about it and walked out of the shop, her cheeks flushed.

It was crazy to feel this way about him, Jenna thought faintly. A man like him wasn't going to be interested in a divorced woman with a teenage daughter. And anyway, for all she knew he could be involved with someone. She couldn't imagine that a man like him could possibly be single.

Frustrated with herself, she hurried to her bike. She had to stop thinking about him. Even if he were interested in her, she wouldn't follow it through. For a start being with him would make her so nervous she wouldn't be able to eat a morsel, and to top it off Lexi was only just starting to settle into her new life. She could just imagine her daughter's reaction if her mother started seeing a man.

Thinking about Ryan occupied her mind for the cycle home, and she was still thinking about him as she propped her bike against the wall of the cottage and picked some flowers from the garden.

She walked into the kitchen to find Lexi sprawled on the kitchen floor, playing with Rebel.

Jenna put the flowers in a vase. 'How was the archae-ology dig today?' Despite her complaints, it had taken Lexi only a matter of days to settle in and start enjoying herself. 'Did you have fun?'

'Yeah. Fraser found a piece of pot—everyone was really excited. I'm going to meet him for a walk on the beach later. I'll take Rebel. What time are we eating? I'm starving.'

Fraser? Lexi wanted to go for a walk on the beach with a boy?

'We're eating in about twenty minutes. So...' Retrieving

the salmon fillets from her bag, Jenna tried to keep her voice casual. 'You haven't mentioned Fraser before. Is he nice?'

'He has a nose ring, five tattoos, long hair and swears all the time.' Lexi rubbed Rebel's glossy fur with her hands. 'You're going to love him—isn't she, Reb?'

With a wry smile, Jenna put the salmon under the grill. 'Lexi, you wait until you're a worried mother—'

'I'm not going to be like you. I'm going to trust my kids.'

Jenna sensed this was one of those moments when it was imperative to say the right thing. 'I trust you, Lexi,' she said quietly. 'You're a bright, caring, funny girl. But you're still a child—'

'I'm nearly sixteen—you're so over-protective.'

'I care about you. And you *are* still a child. Child going on woman, but still… I know all this has been hard on you. And being a teenager isn't easy.'

'What? You remember that far back?' But Lexi was smiling as she picked up Rebel's bowl. 'We're having fish again? I'm going to start swapping meals with the dog.'

'I thought you liked fish.'

'I do. But you never used to cook it in London. Now we have it almost every meal!'

'I didn't cook it in London because Dad hated it.' But Clive wasn't here now, and she was cooking what she wanted. And loving it, Jenna mused, mixing a teriyaki sauce to add to the salmon.

'Given that you're into all this healthy lifestyle stuff, I assume I *can* go for a walk on the beach with Fraser later?'

Jenna felt as though she was treading over broken glass. If she said no, she'd be accused of not trusting, and that could trigger a rebellious response. If she said yes, she'd worry all evening. 'Yes,' she croaked, washing a handful of tomatoes and adding them to the salad. 'All I ask is that you're home before dark.'

'Why? I can have sex in daylight just as easily as in the dark.'

Jenna closed her eyes. 'Lexi—'

'But I'm not going to. Credit me with some sense, Mum. You know I'm not going to do that. You've given me the sex, love, marriage talk often enough.'

'You've got it in the wrong order,' Jenna said weakly. 'And you've missed out contraception.' It was impossible not to be aware that Lexi was only a couple of years younger than she had been when she'd become pregnant.

Lexi rolled her eyes and then walked over and hugged her. 'Just chill, Mum.'

Astonished by the unexpected show of affection, Jenna felt a lump in her throat. 'That's nice. A hug.'

'Yeah—well, I'm sorry I was difficult about moving here. It's a pretty cool place. I didn't mean to be a nightmare.'

Jenna felt a rush of relief. 'You're not a nightmare, baby. I'm glad you're settling in.'

'It would be great if you could worry less.'

'It would be great if you could give me less to worry about.'

'OK. If I'm going to do something really bad, I'll warn you.'

'Lexi—about Fraser…'

'If you're going to talk to me about boys, Mum, don't waste your time. I probably know more than you anyway.'

Jenna blinked. That was probably true. She'd only ever had one boyfriend, and she'd married him at eighteen.

And he'd left her at thirty-two.

Lexi stole a tomato from the salad. 'We're just friends, OK? Mates. He's really easy to talk to. He really *gets* stuff. His dad—' She broke off and then shrugged. 'His dad walked out, too. When he was nine. That's why his mum came here.'

'Oh…'

What had happened to her had happened to millions of women around the world. She wasn't the only one in this situation. Lives shattered and were mended again, and she was mending, wasn't she? Slowly. She stared at the dog lying on her kitchen floor, and the bunch of flowers on her kitchen table. Life was different, but that didn't mean it wasn't good.

'You can go for a walk on the beach, Lexi.'

Lexi visibly relaxed. 'Thanks. We're just going to hang out, that's all. Fraser says there's really cool stuff on the beach once the tide goes out. He knows the names of everything. I feel like a real townie.'

'You'll have to teach me. Have they dug up anything else interesting at the castle yet?'

'Bits of stuff. They found these Viking combs—weird to think of Vikings combing their hair.'

'Perhaps their mothers nagged them,' Jenna said dryly, hugely relieved that Lexi appeared to be more like her old self. 'What's the castle like? I must go up there.'

'It's awesome. Fraser showed me this steep shaft into the dungeons. He fell down it a few years ago and had to have his head stitched up.'

'It sounds dangerous.'

'Only to you. You see danger everywhere.'

'I'm a mother. Worrying goes with the territory.'

'Fraser's mother doesn't fuss over him all the time. She just lets him live his life.'

Jenna bit her lip, trying not to be hurt, well used to being told what other mothers did. 'I'm letting you live your life. I'd just rather you didn't do it in a hospital or an antenatal clinic. Wash your hands, Lex—dinner is nearly ready.'

'Do you want me to lay the table or do drinks or something?'

Hiding her surprise, Jenna smiled at her. 'That would be a great help. There's lemonade in the fridge—Evanna gave it to us as a gift.'

'It's delicious. I had some at her house.' Lexi opened the fridge door again and pulled out the bottle. 'She makes it by the bucketload, all fresh lemons and stuff. She's a good cook.

I told her you were, too. Are we going to the barbecue on Saturday, Mum?'

Still reeling from the compliment, Jenna turned the salmon. 'How do you know about the barbecue?'

'Fraser mentioned it.'

Fraser, Fraser, Fraser—

Still, at least Lexi seemed happy. Relieved, Jenna put the salmon on the plates. 'Do you want to go?'

'Why not? Might be a laugh.' Her eyes narrowed. 'How did *you* hear about the barbecue?'

'In the fishmonger's.' Jenna omitted to say who she'd bumped into there. 'It's amazing to be able to buy such fresh fish.'

'It's amazing what old people find exciting.' Lexi suppressed a yawn as she picked up her plate. 'Let's eat in the garden. So how many lives did you save today? Did you see Dr Hot?'

'Dr who?'

'Dr Hot. Ryan McKinley. I bet women who are perfectly well make appointments just to spend five minutes with him. Fraser says he's brilliant.'

Even at home there was no escape, Jenna thought weakly, taking her plate and following her daughter out into the sunshine.

She wasn't going to think of him as Dr Hot.

She really wasn't.

'She was playing on the deck with a water pistol and she slipped and crashed into the fence—the bruise is horrendous. I'm worried she's fractured her eye socket or something.' The woman's face was white. 'I tried to get an appointment with one of the doctors, but Dr McNeil is out on a call and Dr McKinley has a full list.'

Jenna gave her shoulder a squeeze. 'Let me take a look at it. If I think she needs to be seen by one of the doctors, then I'll arrange it. Hello, Lily.' She crouched down so that she was at the same level as the child. 'What have you been doing to yourself?'

She studied the livid bruise across the child's cheekbone and the swelling distorting the face. 'Was she knocked out?'

'No.' The woman hovered. 'I put an ice pack on it straight away, but it doesn't seem to have made a difference.'

'I'm sure it helped.' Jenna examined the child's cheek, tested her vision and felt the orbit. 'Can you open your mouth for me, Lily? Good girl—now, close—brilliant. Does that hurt?' Confident that there was no fracture, she turned to Lily's mother. 'I think it's just badly bruised, Mrs Parsons.'

'But she could have fractured it. Sorry—it isn't that I don't trust you.' The woman closed her eyes briefly. 'And I know I'm being anxious, but—'

'I know all about anxious. You don't have to apologise.' Seeing how distressed the mother was, and sympathising, Jenna made a decision. 'I'll ask Dr McKinley to check her for you. Then you won't be going home, worrying.'

'Would you?'

'I'll go and see if he's free—just wait one moment.' Giving Lily a toy to play with, Jenna left her room and walked across to Ryan just as the door to his consulting room opened and a patient walked out.

She paused for a moment, conscious that she hadn't seen him since Hamish had embarrassed them both the day before.

'Ryan?' Putting that out of her mind, Jenna put her head round the door. 'I'm sorry, I know you're busy...' And tired, she thought, looking at the shadows under his eyes. He worked harder than any doctor she'd ever met.

Or were the shadows caused by something else?

'I'm not busy—what can I do for you?' The moment he looked at her, Jenna felt her insides flip over.

'I have a patient in my room—I wondered if you could give me your opinion. The little girl is six—she's slipped and banged her face. The bruising is bad, but I don't think there's a fracture—there's no flattening of the cheek.'

Work always helped, she thought. After Clive had left, work had been her healing potion. It had stopped her thinking, analysing, asking 'what if?' And she'd discovered that if you worked hard enough, you fell into bed dog-tired and slept, instead of lying awake, thinking all the same things you'd been thinking during the day.

'Flattening of the cheek can be obscured by swelling—'

'It isn't that swollen yet. It only happened half an hour ago, and her mum put an ice pack on it immediately. I can't feel any defect to the orbit, and she can open and close her mouth without difficulty.'

'It sounds as though you're confident with your assessment.' His long fingers toyed with the pen on his desk. 'Why do you need me?'

'Because the mother is so, so worried. I thought some re-assurance from you might help. I know what it's like to be a panicking mother.'

'Who is the patient?'

'Parsons?'

Ryan stood up. 'Lily Parsons? That explains why you have a worried mother in your room. Little Lily had a nasty accident a couple of years ago—almost died. She fell in deep water in the quay and a boat propeller caught her artery.'

'Oh, no—' Jenna lifted her hand to her throat, horrified by the image his words created. 'How did she survive that?'

'My predecessor, Connor McNeil—Logan's cousin—was ex-army. Trauma was his speciality, otherwise I doubt Lily would be with us today. She went into respiratory arrest, lost so much blood—'

'Were you here?'

'No. It was just before I arrived, but Connor's rescue has gone down in island folklore. Apparently Jayne totally flipped. She witnessed the whole thing—blamed herself for the fact that Lily had fallen in. The child was watching the fish, and a crowd of tourists queuing for the ferry bumped into her and she lost her balance.'

'Poor Jayne!' To stop herself looking at his mouth, Jenna walked back towards the door. 'All the more reason why you should reassure her.'

Without arguing, Ryan followed her into the room, charmed Jayne, made Lily laugh, and then checked the child's eye with a thoroughness that would have satisfied the most hyper-anxious mother.

Jenna watched, wondering why someone with his own trauma skills would give up a glittering career to bury himself on Glenmore.

Something must have happened.

Life, she thought, had a way of doling out grim surprises.

'You're right that there is no flattening of the cheek.' He addressed the remark to Jenna, gave the little girl a wink and strolled across the room to wash his hands. 'Jayne, I'm happy with her, but that bruising is going to get worse before it gets better, and so is the swelling. I'm guessing your worrying is going to get worse before it gets better, too. I'll have a word with Janet on Reception so that she knows to slot you in if you feel worried and want me to take another look.'

'You don't want to X-ray her?'

'No. I don't think it's necessary.' Ryan dried his hands and dropped the paper towel in the bin. 'Look, why don't you bring her back to my surgery tomorrow morning anyway? That will stop you having to look at her every five minutes and decide whether you need to bring her back.'

Jayne Parsons gave a weak smile. 'You must think I'm a total idiot.'

'On the contrary, I think you're a worried mum and that's understandable.' Ryan scribbled a number on a scrap of paper.

'This is my mobile number. I drive past your house on the way to and from the surgery—just give me a call if you're worried and I can drop in. Take care, Lily.'

Mother and child left the room, more relaxed, and Jenna stared at the door. 'Do you give your mobile number to every anxious patient?'

'If I think they need the reassurance, yes. Glenmore is an isolated island. It makes people more reliant on each other. They're in and out of each other's lives.' He gave a faint smile. 'As I'm sure you've noticed.'

She swallowed. 'I'm sorry about Evanna and Hamish—'

'Why are you sorry? None of it is your fault.' Ryan sat down at her desk and brought Lily's notes up on the computer screen. 'They just can't help themselves. Matchmaking is like eating and breathing to the people of Glenmore.'

'It happens a lot?'

'All the time—although I've pretty much escaped it up until now. That's one of the advantages of being a doctor. There are a limited number of people on this island who technically aren't my patients.'

'I expect they'll back off soon.'

'I wouldn't count on it.' Ryan typed the notes with one finger. 'Do you want a lift to the beach barbecue? I could pick you up on my way past.'

'I haven't even decided if we're going.'

'If you don't go, they'll come and get you. Come. Lexi would enjoy it. All the teenagers go. She seems to have made friends. Whenever I see her, she's smiling.'

'Yes.' Jenna was starting to wonder whether there was something more to her daughter's sudden change of attitude. 'What do you know about a boy called Fraser?'

'Fraser Price?' Ryan stood up. 'He lives near you. Just along the beach. His mum is called Ailsa—she's a single parent. Diabetic. Why are you asking?'

Jenna chewed her lip. 'Lexi seems to like him—'

'And you're worrying that he has unsavoury habits?'

'I'm just worrying generally. In London, Lexi started mixing with the wrong crowd. She made a point of doing all the things she thought would upset me…'

'Why would she want to upset you?'

Jenna hesitated. 'She blames me for not trying to fix my marriage.'

'Did you want to fix it?'

Jenna thought about Clive and the scene in his office that day. *Thought about what she'd learned about her marriage.* 'No. Some things can't be fixed.' She had an urge to qualify that with an explanation, but realised that there was no way she could elaborate without revealing that her husband hadn't found her sexy. Somehow that was too humiliating. She turned away and put a box of dressings back into the cupboard. 'There's nothing to talk about. My marriage ended. It happens to thousands of people every day.'

And thousands of people got on with their lives, as she had done. Picking up the pieces, patching them together again into something different.

'Did you think about buying him out so that you could stay in the house?'

It was a practical question, typically male. 'I'm a nurse, Ryan, not a millionaire. London is expensive. And anyway, I didn't want to stay in that house. It was full of memories I didn't want. I knew if I'd stayed there I'd always be looking back. I wanted to move forward. He offered me a sum of money and I took it.'

'I'm guessing it wasn't a generous sum.' His eyes darkened, and she wondered why he'd be angry about something that wasn't his problem.

'He completely ripped me off.' Only now, after almost a year, could she say it without starting to shake with emotion.

'I was really stupid and naïve, but in my own defence I was in a bit of a state at the time. I was more wrapped up in the emotional than the practical. I shouldn't really have been negotiating a divorce settlement so soon after he'd walked out. There were some mornings when I couldn't bear to drag myself from under the duvet. If it hadn't been for Lexi I wouldn't have bothered. I left it to him to get the valuations. And he took advantage.' She lifted her chin. 'He used his friends—fiddled with the numbers and offered me a sum that was just about plausible. And I took it. So I'm to blame for being a push-over.'

'You weren't a push-over. You were in shock, and I'm guessing you just wanted it to end.'

'I didn't want it dragging on and hurting Lexi. The whole thing was very hard on her.' Jenna rubbed her hands up and down her arms. 'And she was so angry with me.'

He took a slow breath. 'You did a brave thing, coming here. Was it the right thing to do?'

She considered the question. 'Yes. Yes, it was. We're healing.' The discovery warmed her. 'The best thing I did was to get Rebel. Lexi adores him. So do I. And we love living in the cottage. Having the beach on our doorstep is like heaven. And I'm relieved Lexi is happy, although I'm worrying that has something to do with her new friend.'

'I don't think you have to worry about Fraser. He's pretty responsible.'

'Well, if he's the reason Lexi is happy, then I suppose he has my approval.'

Ryan strolled towards the door. His arm brushed against hers and Jenna felt the response shoot right through her body. Seeing the frown touch his forehead, she wondered if he did, too.

'Our receptionist Janet was saying how smoothly everything is running since you arrived. The islanders love you.'

'Everyone has been very kind.' She wondered why she felt

compelled to look at him all the time. If he was in the room, she wanted to stare. Every bit of him fascinated her, from his darkened jaw to his thick, lustrous hair. But what really interested her was him. The man.

She wanted to ask why he'd chosen to come to Glenmore, but there was something about him that didn't invite personal questions.

Respecting his privacy, she smiled. 'We'll see you at the barbecue on Saturday.'

'Good.' He watched her for a long moment and she felt that look all the way down to her bones.

'Thanks for seeing Lily.'

He stirred. 'You're welcome.'

The sun was just breaking through the early-morning mist when she walked Rebel early the following day. The garden gate no longer creaked, thanks to a regular dose of oil, and Jenna paused for a moment to admire the pinks and purples in her garden before walking along the sandy path that led through the dunes to the beach. The stretch of sand was deserted and she slipped off her shoes and walked barefoot, loving the feel of the sand between her toes. Rebel bounded ahead, investigating pieces of seaweed and driftwood, tail wagging. Every now and then he raced back to her, sending water and sand flying.

Huge foaming breakers rolled in from the Atlantic, rising high and then exploding onto the beach with a crash and a hiss. Jenna watched as a lone surfer achieved apparently impossible feats in the deadly waves. Admiring his strength and the fluidity of his body, she gave herself a little shake and turned her attention to the beach. After twenty years of not noticing men, suddenly she seemed to do nothing else.

Seeing a pretty shell poking out of the sand, she stooped to pick it up. The pearly white surface peeped from beneath a layer of sand and she carefully brushed it and slipped it into her pocket, thinking of the chunky glass vase in her little bathroom, which was already almost full of her growing collection of shells.

She was pocketing her second shell when Rebel started to bark furiously. He sped across the sand towards the water just as the surfer emerged from the waves, his board under his arm.

Recognising Ryan, Jenna felt her heart bump hard against her chest and she forgot about shells. She should have known it was him from the visceral reaction deep in her stomach. It wasn't men in general she was noticing. It was just one man.

Without thinking, she dragged her fingers through her curls and then recognised the futility of the gesture. She was wearing an old pair of shorts and a cotton tee shirt. Running her fingers through her hair wasn't going to make her presentable. For a moment she regretted not spending a few moments in front of the mirror before leaving her cottage. Thinking of herself doing her morning walk in lipgloss and a pretty top made her smile, and she was still smiling when he ran up to her.

'What's funny?'

'Meeting someone else at this time of the morning.'

He put his surfboard down on the sand. 'It's the best time. I surf most mornings, but I've never seen you out before.' The wetsuit emphasised the width and power of his shoulders and she looked towards the waves, trying to centre herself.

'Normally I'm a little later than this but I couldn't sleep.' Because she'd been thinking about him. And then pushing away those thoughts with rational argument. But now those thoughts were back, swirling round her head, confusing her.

'You couldn't sleep?' His tone was amused. 'Maybe you were excited about the barbecue tomorrow.'

'That must have been it.' As Rebel bounded up to her, she

sidestepped, dodging the soaking wet tail-wagging animal. 'Sit. *Sit!*' Ignoring her, Rebel shook himself hard and sprayed them both. 'Oh, you—! Rebel! I'm so sorry.'

'More of a problem for you than me. I'm wearing a wet-suit.' His eyes drifted to her damp tee shirt and lingered. 'Obviously the dog-training is progressing successfully.'

'It's a disaster. He obeyed me that day at Elaine's just to charm me into giving him a home. Since then he's been a nightmare.' Giggling and embarrassed, Jenna grabbed Rebel's collar and glared at him severely. 'Sit! Sit, Rebel. I said sit!'

The dog whimpered, his entire body wagging, and Ryan sighed.

'Sit!'

Rebel sat.

'OK—that's annoying.' Jenna put her hands on her hips. 'I've been working non-stop with him and you just say it once. What do you have that I don't?'

'An air of menace. You're kind and gentle. A dog can sense you're soft-hearted. Especially a dog like Rebel, who has had his own way for far too long.'

'You think I'm a push-over?'

'I don't see you as tough and ruthless, that's true.'

Her heart was pounding as if she'd run the length of the beach. 'I'll have you know I'm stronger than I look!'

'I didn't say you weren't strong.' The pitch of his voice had changed. 'I know you're strong, Jenna. You've proved your strength over and over again in the last month. You've dragged up your roots and put them down somewhere new. That's never easy.'

His eyes were oceans of blue, waiting to draw her in and drown her.

The want inside her became a desperate craving, and when his arm curled around her waist and he drew her towards him she didn't resist. Her thinking went from clear to clouded, and she waited, deliciously trapped by the inevitability of what was to come. She watched, hypnotised, as he lowered his head to hers. His mouth was warm and skilled, his kiss sending an explosion of light through her brain and fire through her belly.

It should have felt wrong, kissing a man. But it felt right—standing here with his lips against hers and nothing around them but the sound and smell of the sea.

Jenna dug her fingers into the front of his wetsuit, felt the hardness of his body brush against her knuckles. The fire spread, licking its way through her limbs until she was unsteady on her feet, and his grip on her tightened, his mouth more demanding as they kissed hungrily, feasting, exploring, discovering.

Rebel barked.

Ryan lifted his mouth from hers, his reluctance evident in the time he took. Dazed and disorientated, Jenna stared up at him for a moment and then at his mouth.

Now she knew how it felt...

Rebel barked again and she turned her head, trying to focus on the dog.

'What's the matter with you?' Her voice was croaky and Ryan released her.

'People on the beach.' His voice was calm and steady. 'Clearly we're not the only early risers.'

'Obviously not.' She knew she sounded stilted but she had no idea what to say. Were they supposed to talk about it? Or pretend it had never happened? 'I should be getting home. Lexi will be waking up...' Feeling really strange, she lifted a shaking hand to her forehead. The kiss had changed everything. Her world had tilted.

'Jenna—'

'I'll see you tomorrow.'

His gaze was disturbingly acute. 'You'll see me at the surgery today.'

'Yes—yes, of course I will. That's what I meant.' Flustered, she called to Rebel, who was nosing something on the sand, apparently oblivious to the fact that his owner's life had just changed.

Ryan seemed about to say something, but the people on the beach were moving closer and he shook his head in exasperation. 'I've never seen anyone else on this beach at this hour.'

'It's a very pretty place.' Babbling, Jenna backed away. 'You'd better go and have a shower—warm up—you can't do a surgery in your wetsuit—I really ought to be going—' She would have tripped over Rebel if Ryan hadn't shot out a hand and steadied her. 'Thanks. I'll see you later.' Without looking at him, she turned and almost flew over the sand after Rebel, not pausing until she was inside the cottage with the door shut firmly behind her.

'Mum? What's the matter with you?' Yawning, Lexi stood there in tee shirt and knickers.

'I've been—' Kissed, Jenna thought hysterically. Thoroughly, properly, deliciously kissed. '—for a walk. On the beach. With Rebel.'

Lexi threw her an odd look. 'Well, of course with Rebel—who else?'

'No one else. Absolutely no one else.' She needed to shut up before she said something she regretted. 'You're up early.'

'I'm going over to Evanna's to give the children breakfast before I go to the dig. She has that appointment thing today on the mainland so she took the first ferry.'

'Yes, of course. I know. I remember.' Her lips felt warm and tingly, and if she really concentrated she could still conjure up the feel of his mouth against hers. 'I have to take a shower and get ready for work.'

'Are you all right? You look—different.'

She felt different.

Up until today she'd felt as though she was surviving. Now she felt as though she was living.

Everything was different.

CHAPTER SIX

Too dressy.

Too casual.

Too cold—

Jenna threw the contents of her wardrobe onto her bed and stared at it in despair. Was it really that hard to decide what to wear to a beach barbecue? It was so long since she'd been out socially she'd lost her confidence. But she knew that the real reason she couldn't decide what to wear was because Ryan would be there and she wanted to look her best. Without looking as though she'd tried too hard.

Infuriated with herself, she reached for the first skirt she'd tried on, slipped it over her head and picked a simple tee shirt to go with it. The skirt was pretty, but the tee shirt was plain— which meant that the top half of her was underdressed and the bottom half was overdressed.

Looking in the mirror, Jenna scooped up her hair and piled it on top of her head. Then she pulled a face and let it fall loose around her shoulders. She gave a hysterical giggle. Maybe she should wear half of it up and half of it down.

'Mum?'

Hearing Lexi's voice, Jenna jumped guiltily and scooped the discarded clothes from the bed. She was just closing the wardrobe door on the evidence of her indecision when Lexi sauntered into the room.

'Are you ready?'

'Nearly.' Jenna eyed the lipgloss that she'd bought. It was still in its packaging because she hadn't decided whether or not to wear it. 'I just need to do my hair.' Up or down?

'Can I go ahead? I'm meeting Fraser.'

'We'll go together,' Jenna said firmly. With no choice but to leave her hair down, she grabbed a cardigan and made for the stairs. 'I'd like to meet him.'

'We're just mates,' Lexi muttered, sliding her feet into a pair of pretty flip-flops. 'We're not quite at the "meet the parents" stage.'

Jenna picked up her keys and the bowl containing the strawberries. 'This is Glenmore. On an island this size you have no option but to meet the parents. Everyone meets everyone about five times a day.' She wished she hadn't left her hair down. It made her feel wild and unrestrained, and she wanted to feel restrained and together.

'Are you all right, Mum?'

'I'm fine. Why wouldn't I be?'

'I don't know…' Her phone in her hand, Lexi frowned. 'You just seem jumpy. Nervous. You've been acting really weird since yesterday.'

'Nervous? I have no reason to be nervous!'

'All right, calm down. I realise it's a big excitement for you, getting out for an evening. Don't be too embarrassing, will you?'

Jenna locked the door because she hadn't got out of the London habit. 'I'm meant to be the one saying that to you.'

'Going out with your mother would never happen in London. Just promise me that whatever happens you won't dance.'

Ryan watched her walk across the sand towards him.

She'd left her hair loose, the way she'd worn it on the day she'd arrived on the island.

Feeling the tension spread across his shoulders, he lifted the bottle of beer to his lips, thinking about the kiss. He hadn't intended to kiss her but the temptation had been too great, and now he couldn't get it out of his mind.

He wondered why this woman in particular should have such a powerful effect on him. Not for one moment did he think it was anything to do with her gorgeous curves—he'd met plenty of women with good bodies and none of them had tempted him past the superficial. But Jenna...

Maybe it was her generous smile. Or her air of vulnerability—the way she was so painfully honest about the things that had gone wrong in her life when most people just put up a front. Or the way she put herself last. Either way, she was sneaking under his skin in a way that should have set off warning bells.

If his aim was to protect himself, then lusting after a recently divorced single mother with a teenage daughter was probably the stupidest thing he'd ever done.

She was clearly desperately hurt after her divorce, and any relationship she entered into now would be on the rebound.

But his body wasn't listening to reason and he felt himself harden as he watched her approach. She'd dressed modestly, her summery skirt falling to her ankles, her tee shirt high at the neck. But the Glenmore breeze was designed to mock modesty and it flattened the skirt to her legs, found the slit and blew it gaily until the soft fabric flew into the air, revealing long slim legs and a hint of turquoise that looked like a swimming costume.

Ryan saw her clutch at the skirt and drag it back into position, her face pink as she pinned it down with her hand, defying the wind.

For a girl who was fresh out of the city, there was nothing city-slick about her. She was carrying a large flowery bag over one shoulder and she looked slightly uncertain—as if she wasn't used to large gatherings.

He was fully aware that she'd avoided him the day before at the surgery, going to great lengths to make sure they didn't bump into one another. Seeing her now, the emotion he felt was like a punch in the gut. He was attracted to her in a way he hadn't been attracted to a woman in years.

'She'd be perfect for you.' Evanna's voice came from behind him and he turned, keeping his expression neutral.

'You never give up, do you?'

'Not when I think something is worth the effort.' Evanna replied. 'Don't be angry with me.'

'Then don't interfere.'

'I'm helping.'

'Do you think I need help?'

'When you first came here, yes. You were so angry,' she said softly. 'I used to hear you sawing wood and banging nails. You swung that hammer as if you hoped someone's head was underneath it.'

Ryan breathed out slowly. 'I hadn't realised anyone witnessed that—'

'I came down to the lighthouse from time to time, trying to pluck up courage to ask you to join us for supper, but whenever I saw you your expression was so black and you were so dark and scary I lost my nerve.'

'I didn't know.' He'd been aware of nothing, he realised, but his own pain. 'So, have you become braver or am I less scary?'

Her smile was wise and gentle. 'You banged in a lot of nails.'

'I guess I did.' He respected the fact that she hadn't pushed him for the reason. She'd never pushed him. Just offered unconditional friendship. Humbled once again by the generosity of the islanders, he frowned. 'Evanna—'

'Just promise me that if I back off you won't let her slip through your fingers.'

'Life doesn't always come as neatly wrapped as you seem to think.'

'It takes work to wrap something neatly.' She stood on tiptoe and kissed his cheek. 'You've been here for two years. It's enough. Don't let the past mess up the future, Ryan.'

'Is that what I'm doing?'

'I don't know. Are you?'

Ryan thought about the kiss on the beach and the way he felt about Jenna. 'No,' he said. 'I'm not.'

He knew Jenna was nothing like Connie. And maybe that was one of the reasons he was so attracted to her.

'Is my wife sorting out your love-life?' Logan strolled over to them, Charlie on his shoulders.

'Who? Me?' Her expression innocent, Evanna picked up a bowl of green salad. 'Can you put this on the table, please? Next to the tomato salsa. I'm going to meet Jenna and make her feel welcome. She looks nervous. I'm sure she feels a bit daunted by the crowd.'

Ryan was willing to bet that her nerves had nothing to do with the crowd and everything to do with the kiss they'd shared. He'd flustered her.

He gave a faint smile. And he was looking forward to flustering her again.

'What does tomato salsa look like?' Logan's expression was comical as he steadied Charlie with one hand and took the salad from Evanna with the other. 'Is that the mushy red stuff?' Leaning forward, he kissed her swiftly on the mouth and Evanna sighed and kissed him back.

Watching them together, seeing the soft looks and the way they touched, Ryan felt a stab of something sharp stab his gut and recognised it as envy.

Even in the early days, his relationship with Connie had never been like that. They'd never achieved that level of closeness. They'd been a disaster waiting to happen. If he hadn't been so absorbed by his career maybe he would have picked up on the signs. Or maybe not. Connie had played her part well.

Lifting the bottle to his lips again, he watched as Evanna sprinted across the sand to meet Jenna—watched as she gave her a spontaneous hug and gestured with her hands, clearly telling her some anecdote. He had no idea what she was saying, but it had Jenna laughing, and her laugh was so honest and genuine that Ryan felt every muscle in his body tighten. He doubted Jenna had ever manipulated a man in her life. She wouldn't know how—and anyway, such behaviour would go against her moral code.

As they approached he could hear Evanna admiring Jenna's skirt, the conversation light and distinctly female in tone and content. Jenna responded in kind, handing over a bowl of rosy-red strawberries and chatting with the group gathered around the food table as if she'd been born and raised on the island.

It took less than a few seconds for him to realise that she was looking at everyone but him. Talking to everyone but him.

Aware of Evanna's puzzled expression, Ryan sighed. If he didn't do something, the situation would be taken out of his hands.

He strolled over to Jenna, who was busily sorting food on the long trestle table, carefully ignoring him.

'Where's Rebel?' Ryan felt the ripple of tension pass through her body and she carefully put down the bowl she was holding.

'Lexi has him on a lead. I thought all those sausages and steaks on the barbecue might prove too much of a temptation for a dog with a behavioural problem.'

'You could be right.' He noticed that her cheeks had turned a soft shade of pink and that she was making a point of not looking at his mouth.

No, he thought to himself. Jenna would never play games or manipulate. She was honest and genuine—surprisingly unsophisticated for a woman in her thirties.

Lexi strolled up to the table, earphones hanging from her ears, her iPod tucked into the back pocket of her jeans, her head bobbing to the rhythm. She was hanging on to Rebel, who was straining to run in the opposite direction. 'Hi, Ryan.'

Jenna looked embarrassed. 'Dr McKinley—'

'Ryan is fine.' He bent down to make a fuss of Rebel, who looked him in the eye and immediately sat.

'Mum, did you see that? He sat without even being told!' Lexi gaped at the dog. 'Given that he's behaving, you can hold him. I'm going to see my friends.' Without waiting for a reply, she pushed the lead into her mother's hand, took the cola Evanna was offering her with a smile of thanks and strolled across the sand to join a group of teenagers who were chatting together.

'I have a feeling it was a mistake to bring a dog—this particular dog, anyway—to a barbecue.' Gripping the lead until her knuckles were white, Jenna was still concentrating on Rebel. 'Hopefully your influence will prevail and he'll behave.'

'I think you may have an exaggerated idea of my power.'

'I hope not or I'm about to be seriously embarrassed.'

'I think you're already embarrassed.' Ryan spoke quietly, so that he couldn't be overheard by the people milling close to them. Keeping his eyes on her face, he watched her reaction. 'And there's no need to be. Just as there was no need to run off yesterday morning and avoid me all day in surgery.'

She took a deep breath, her gaze fixed on Rebel. Then she glanced sideways and checked no one was listening. Finally, she looked at him. 'I haven't kissed, or been kissed, for a long time.'

'I know.' He watched as the tension rippled down her spine.

'I wasn't sure how I felt about it— I mean—' Her colour deepened. 'Obviously I know how I felt, but I wasn't sure what it all meant. I hadn't expected—'

'Neither had I.' Suddenly he regretted starting this conversation in such a public place. He should have dragged her somewhere private where he could have matched actions with words.

'Everyone is trying to pair us up.'

'I know that, too.'

'Doesn't that put you off?'

'I didn't kiss you because it was what other people wanted, Jenna. I kissed you because it was what I wanted.' And he still wanted it, he realised. Badly. Maybe two years of self-imposed isolation had intensified his feelings, but he had a feeling that it was something more than that.

'Is everyone watching us now?'

'Ignore them. What can I get you to drink?'

'What are you drinking?'

'Ginger beer,' he said dryly, 'but I'm on call. How about a glass of wine?'

She hesitated for a moment, and then something sparked in her eyes. 'Actually, I'd like a beer,' she said firmly. 'From the bottle. Don't bother with a glass.'

Hiding his surprise, Ryan took a bottle of ice-cold beer from the cooler and handed it to her. Maybe he didn't know her as well as he thought. She certainly didn't strike him as a woman who drank beer from a bottle.

'Thanks. Cheers.' Her grin was that of a defiant child, and she took a large mouthful and proceeded to spill half of it down her front. 'Oh, for goodness' sake!'

Struggling to keep a straight face, Ryan rescued her beer before she spilt the rest of it. 'You haven't done that before, have you?'

Pulling a face, she tugged her wet tee shirt away from her chest. 'What a mess! Everyone is going to think I'm an alcoholic.'

'Alcoholics generally manage to get the alcohol into their mouths, Jenna. I gather your husband was more of a wine in a glass sort of guy?' Ryan put their drinks down on the table and grabbed a handful of paper napkins.

'How do you know what my husband drank?'

'It's a wild guess, based on the fact you seem to be doing the opposite of everything you ever did with him.' He pressed the napkins against the damp patch, feeling the swell of her breasts under his fingers.

'Am I?'

'You got yourself a dog, you're drinking beer from the bottle for the first time in your life, you eat fish three times a week and you never used to eat fish—' He could have added that she'd kissed a man who wasn't her husband, but he decided it was better to leave that alone for now.

'How do you know how often I eat fish?'

'Hamish mentioned it.'

Her gasp was an astonished squeak. 'The islanders discuss my diet?'

'The islanders discuss everything. You should know that by now.'

'In that case you should probably let me mop up my own wet tee shirt.' She snatched the napkins from his hands, their fingers brushing. 'If we're trying to kill the gossip, I don't think you should be doing that.'

'Do you care about the gossip?'

'I care about Lexi hearing the gossip.'

'Ah—' He noticed the pulse beating in her throat and knew she felt the attraction as strongly as he did. He retrieved his bottle from the table. 'Can I get you something different to drink?'

'Absolutely not.' There was humour in her eyes. And determination. 'I'm not a quitter. If you can drink from the bottle without dribbling, then so can I.' She lifted the bottle carefully to her lips and this time didn't spill a drop.

His body throbbing, Ryan stood close to her. 'You were late. I thought you weren't coming.'

'I was working in the garden, and then Lexi had to change her outfit four times. And I wasn't sure if it was a good idea…' She paused, staring at the label on the bottle. 'This stuff is disgusting.'

'It's an acquired taste. And now?'

'I still don't know if it's a good idea. I've never been so confused in my life.'

Evanna was back at the table, rearranging salads and plates. Ryan saw the happy smile on her lips and ground his teeth. Suddenly he felt protective—Jenna ought to be able to get out and spread her wings socially without being made to feel that everything she did was being analysed and gossiped about.

He was about to intervene when Kirsty, Evanna's six-year-old daughter, sprinted across the sand and launched herself at Lexi. 'Lex—Lex, I want to show you my swimming.'

Ryan watched as the teenager stooped to pick the little girl up. 'Wow. Lucky me. I can't wait to see.' She was a million miles from the moody, sullen teenager who had dragged her feet off the ferry a month before.

The little girl's smile spread right across her face as she bounced in Lexi's arms. 'I can swim without armbands.'

'Really? That's cool.'

'Watch me.'

'Please would you watch me.' Evanna tipped dressing from a jug onto a bowl of salad leaves. 'Manners, Kirsty.'

'Pleeeease—'

Lexi grinned. 'Sure. But don't splash me. It took me ages to get my hair straight.' Her face suddenly turned scarlet, and Ryan glanced round and saw Fraser strolling across the sand towards them, a lopsided grin on his face.

'Hey, if it isn't the city girl.' He wore his board shorts low on his hips and carried a football under his arm. 'We were wondering when you were going to get here. You going to swim for us, Kirst?'

Ryan felt Jenna tense beside him and saw Lexi's shoulders stiffen.

'This is my mum—' She waved a hand awkwardly towards Jenna. 'This is Fraser.'

'Hi, Fraser.' Jenna's voice was friendly. 'Nice to meet you.'

'Hi, Mrs Richards.' With an easy smile Fraser pushed his sun-bleached hair out of his eyes and kicked the football towards his friends. 'Evanna, is it OK if we take Kirsty swimming?'

'You'd be doing me a favour.' Evanna didn't hesitate. 'Don't let her get her own way too often.'

With Kirsty still in her arms, Lexi slid off her shoes and walked barefoot across the sand with Fraser. Close, but not touching.

Watching Jenna sink her teeth into her lower lip, Ryan sighed. 'Relax.'

'Lexi isn't old enough to have responsibility for Kirsty. I'd better follow them.'

He wondered who she was worried about—Kirsty or her own daughter.

'She'll be fine,' Evanna said calmly. 'Fraser is very respon-sible. The beach here is pretty safe, and Ryan can keep an eye on them—he's the strongest swimmer round here.' Smiling, she gave Ryan a little push. 'Go on. You're on lifeguard duty.'

Ryan glanced at Logan, who was expertly flipping steaks on the barbecue.

'Your wife is a bully.'

'I know. I love a strong, forceful woman, don't you?'

It was a flippant remark, with no hidden meaning, but Ryan felt his jaw tighten as he considered the question. He liked a woman to be independent, yes. Strong? He had no problem with strong—he knew from experience that life dealt more blows than a boxer, so strong was probably good. But forceful? Was forceful a euphemism for selfish and single-minded? For doing absolutely what you wanted to do with no thought for anyone else? If so, then the answer was no—he didn't like forceful women.

The question killed his mood, and he was aware that Jenna was looking at him with concern in her eyes.

'I'll keep you company. You made me buy a swimming costume so I might as well use it.' She put her drink down. 'If you're really on lifeguard duty then you can come in the water with me. It's so long since I swam I'm probably going to need my own personal lifeguard.'

Wanting to escape his thoughts, Ryan put his drink down next to hers. 'All right.'

They walked across the sand and she quickened her pace to keep up with him.

'You seem upset.' She kept walking. 'Is something wrong?'

Startled by her insight, Ryan frowned, his eyes on the sea, where Lexi was dangling a shrieking Kirsty in the water. 'What could be wrong?'

'I don't know. I just thought—you seem very tense all of a sudden. I thought maybe you needed some space.' She took a deep breath. 'If you want to talk to someone, you can talk to me.'

Ryan turned his head in astonishment and she bit her lip, her smile faltering.

'I know, I know—men don't like to talk about their problems. But you've listened to me often enough over the past month—I just want you to know that the friendship works both ways.'

'Friendship?' He realised that he was looking at her mouth again, and the strange thing was he didn't need to look. He'd memorised everything about it, from the way her lips curved to the soft pink colour. 'Is that what we have?'

'Of course. I mean, I hope so. You've certainly been a friend to me since I arrived here.'

He stared down into her eyes and something shimmered between them. Something powerful. So powerful that if they hadn't been standing in the middle of a crowded beach with the entire population of Glenmore watching he would have kissed her again.

Unsettled by his own feelings, Ryan shifted his gaze back to the sea. 'I don't have any problems.' His tone was rougher than he'd intended and he heard her sigh.

'You've known me long enough to kiss me, Ryan,' she said quietly. 'Hopefully you've also known me long enough to trust me.'

He was about to say that it was nothing to do with trust, but he was too late. She was already walking ahead, her hair tumbling down her back, sand dusting her toes.

Wondering whether he'd hurt her feelings, Ryan followed her to the water's edge, relieved when she smiled at him.

Clearly Jenna Richards didn't sulk. Nor did she bear grudges.

Fraser and Lexi were either side of Kirsty, holding her hands and swinging her over the waves while she squealed with delight. All of them were laughing.

Ryan was about to speak when he caught the wistful expression on Jenna's face. Her eyes were on Kirsty, and she had that look on her face that women sometimes had when they stared into prams.

He wondered again why she'd only had one child when she was clearly a born mother. Patient, caring, and unfailingly loving.

Pain shafted through him like a lightning bolt and he watched as she lifted her skirt slightly and tentatively allowed the waves to lick her feet. With a soft gasp of shock she jumped back, her eyes shining with laughter as she looked at him.

'It's freezing! Forget swimming. I'll definitely turn to ice and drown if I go in there!'

Forcing aside his dark thoughts, Ryan strode into the waves. 'No way are you using that pathetic excuse.' He took her hand and pulled her deeper. 'You get used to it after a while.'

'After losing how many limbs to frostbite?' Still holding his hand, she lifted her skirt above her knees with her free hand. 'I'm not going to get used to this. I'm losing all sensation in my feet.'

'What are you complaining about?' He tightened his grip on her hand. 'This is a warm evening on Glenmore.'

'The evening may be warm, but someone has forgotten to tell the sea it's summer. My feet are aching they're so cold.' Her laughter was infectious, and Ryan found that he was laughing, too.

Laughing with a woman. That was something he hadn't done for a long time.

He intercepted Lexi's shocked stare and his laughter faded. She glanced between him and her mother, suspicion in her eyes.

Jenna was still laughing as she picked her way through the waves, apparently unaware of her daughter's frozen features.

'We wouldn't be doing this in London, would we, Lex?'

'Pull your skirt down, Mum,' Lexi hissed, and Ryan watched as Jenna suddenly went from being natural to self-conscious. The colour flooded into her cheeks and she released the skirt. Instantly the hem trailed in the water. Flustered, she lifted it again.

'Lexi, watch me, watch me—' Kirsty bounced in the water, but Lexi stepped closer to her mother and dumped the child in Jenna's arms.

'Here you are, Mum. You take her. You're good with kids. Probably because you're old and motherly.'

Ryan was about to laugh at the joke when he realised that no one was laughing.

Old and motherly?

Was that how Lexi saw her mother? Was that how Jenna saw herself?

How old was she? Thirty-two? Thirty-three? She could have passed for ten years younger than that. She had a fresh, natural appeal that he found incredibly sexy. And, yes, she was different from Connie.

His jaw hardened. Connie wouldn't have paddled in the sea—nor would she have appeared in public with a face free of make-up. And he couldn't remember a time when she'd giggled. But that might have been because Connie wasn't spontaneous. She was a woman with a plan and nothing was going to stand in her way. Certainly not their marriage.

'I can't believe you're brave enough to swim!' Jenna was beaming at Kirsty, as if the child had done something incredibly clever. 'I'm so cold I can barely stand in the water, let alone swim.' She sneaked a glance after her daughter, who was walking away from them, Fraser by her side.

'I swim with my daddy.' Keen to demonstrate her skills, Kirsty wriggled in Jenna's arms and plunged back into the water, thrashing her arms and kicking her legs.

Drenched and shivering, Jenna laughed. 'Kirsty, that's fantastic. I couldn't swim like that at your age. And never in sea this cold.' The water had glued the skirt to her legs and Logan looked away, forcing himself to concentrate on something other than the shape of her body.

A crowd of locals were playing volleyball, and he could see Evanna handing out plates of food. 'I smell barbecue,' he said mildly. 'We should probably go and eat something. Sausages, Kirsty?'

The child immediately held out her arms to Jenna, who scooped her out of the water and cuddled her, ignoring the damp limbs and soaking costume.

Ryan felt his body tighten as he watched her with the child.

It was such a painful moment that when the phone in his pocket buzzed he was grateful for the excuse to walk away.

'I'm on call. I'd better take this.' He strode out of the water and drew the phone from his pocket. Was he ever going to be able to look at a mother and child without feeling that degree of agony? He answered his phone with a violent stab of his finger. 'McKinley.' It took him less than five seconds to get the gist of the conversation. 'I'll be right there.' Even as he dropped the phone into this pocket, he was running.

Cuddling a soaking wet Kirsty, Jenna watched as Ryan took off across the beach. It was obvious that there was some sort of emergency. Knowing he'd probably need help, she waded out of the water as fast as her soaked skirt and the bouncing child would allow. Once on the sand, she put the little girl down and ran, holding the child's hand.

'Let's see how fast we can reach Mummy.' At least an emergency might stop her thinking about that kiss. Nothing else had worked so far.

They reached Evanna as she was handing Ryan a black bag.

'What's wrong?' Jenna handed Kirsty over to her mother. 'Is it an emergency?'

Ryan glanced at her briefly. 'Ben who runs the Stag's Head has a tourist who has collapsed. Logan—' He raised his voice. 'I'm going to the pub. Keep your phone switched on.'

'I'll come with you.' Jenna glanced across at Evanna. 'Lexi's walked off with Fraser—will you keep an eye on her for me?'

'Of course.' Looking worried, Evanna held toddler Charlie on her hip and a serving spoon in her other hand. 'I hope it turns out to be nothing. We'll hold the fort here, but if you need reinforcements call.'

Hampered by her wet skirt, Jenna sprinted after Logan and it was only when her feet touched tarmac that she realised she'd left her shoes back at the barbecue. 'Ouch!' Stupid, stupid. 'I left my shoes—'

The next minute she was scooped off the ground and Logan was carrying her across the road.

She gave a gasp of shock. 'Put me down! I weigh a ton!'

'You don't weigh anything, and it's good for my ego to carry a helpless woman occasionally.' He was still jogging, and she realised how fit he must be.

'I'm not helpless, just shoeless.'

'Cinderella.' With a brief smile, he lowered her to the pavement and strode into the pub.

Jenna followed, feeling ridiculous in a wet skirt and without shoes. But all self-consciousness faded as she saw the man lying on the floor. His lips and eyes were puffy, his breathing was laboured and noisy, and the woman next to him was shaking his shoulder and crying.

'Pete? Pete?'

'What happened?' Ryan was down on the floor beside the patient, checking his airway. His fingers moved swiftly and skilfully, checking, eliminating, searching for clues.

'One moment he was eating his supper,' the landlord said, 'and then he crashed down on the floor, holding his throat.'

'He said he felt funny,' his wife sobbed. 'He had a strange feeling in his throat. All of a sudden. I've no idea why. We've been on the beach all afternoon and he was fine. Never said a thing about feeling ill or anything.'

'Anaphylactic shock.' Ryan's mouth was grim and Jenna dropped to her knees beside him.

'Is he allergic to anything?' She glanced at the man's wife. 'Nuts? Could he have been stung? Wasp?'

The woman's eyes were wild with panic. 'I don't think he was stung and he's not allergic to anything. He's fine with nuts, all that sort of stuff—is he going to die?'

Ryan had his hand in his bag. 'He's not going to die. Ben, call the air ambulance and fetch me that oxygen you keep round the back.' Icy calm, he jabbed an injection of adrenaline into the man's thigh, working with astonishing speed. 'Pete? Can you hear me? I'm Dr McKinley.'

Catching a glimpse of the role he'd played in a previous life, Jenna switched her focus back to the man's wife. 'What were you eating?' She looked at the table. 'Fish pie?'

'Yes. But he'd only had a few mouthfuls.'

'Are there prawns in that fish pie?'

'Yes.' Ben was back with the oxygen. 'But they were fresh this morning.'

'I'm not suggesting food poisoning,' Jenna said quickly, 'but maybe shellfish allergy?'

Covering the man's mouth and nose with the oxygen mask, Ryan looked at her for a moment, his eyes narrowed. Then he nodded. 'Shellfish. That's possible. That would explain it.' He adjusted the flow of oxygen. 'I'll give him five minutes and then give him another shot of epinephrine. Can you find it?'

Jenna delved in his bag and found the other drugs they were likely to need.

'Shellfish allergy?' The wife looked at them in horror. 'But—this isn't the first time he's eaten shellfish—can you just develop an allergy like that? Out of nowhere?'

'Jenna, can you squeeze his arm for me? I want to get a line in.'

'Actually, yes.' Jenna spoke to the woman as she handed Ryan a sterile cannula and then watched as he searched for a vein. 'Some adults do develop an allergy to something that hasn't harmed them before.'

'The body just decides it doesn't like it?'

'The body sees it as an invader,' Jenna explained, blinking at the speed with which Ryan obtained IV access. Her fingers over his, she taped down the cannula so that it wouldn't be dislodged, the movements routine and familiar. 'It basically overreacts and produces chemicals and antibodies. Dr McKinley has just given an injection to counter that reaction.'

The woman's face was paper-white. 'Is it going to work?'

'I hope so. This is quite a severe reaction, so I'm giving him another dose.' Ryan took the syringe from Jenna. 'And I'm going to give him some antihistamine and hydrocortisone.'

'Air ambulance is on its way,' Ben said, and at that moment

Jenna noticed something. Leaning forward, she lifted the man's tee shirt so that she could get a better look.

'He has a rash, Ryan.'

'I think it's safe to assume we're dealing with a shellfish allergy—when you get to the mainland they'll observe him overnight and then make an appointment for you to see an allergy consultant. Where do you live?'

'We're from London. We're just here for a holiday. We have another week to go.' The woman was staring at her husband's chest in disbelief. 'I've never seen a rash come on like that.'

'It's all part of the reaction,' Jenna said quietly. 'The drugs will help.'

'How long do you think they'll keep him in hospital?'

'With any luck they'll let you go tomorrow and you can get on with your holiday—avoiding shellfish.' Ryan examined the rash carefully. 'The hospital should refer you for allergy testing so you can be sure what you're dealing with. You may need to carry an Epipen.' He checked the man's pulse again. 'His breathing is improving. That last injection seems to have done the trick.'

'Thank goodness—' The woman slumped slightly and Jenna slipped her arm round her.

'You poor thing. Are you on your own here? Do you have any friends or family with you?' She tried to imagine what it must be like going through this on holiday, far from home, with no support.

'My sister and her husband, but they've gone to the beach barbecue.'

'I'll contact them for you,' Ben said immediately, taking the details and sending one of the locals down to the beach to locate the woman's family.

Once again the islanders impressed Jenna, working together to solve the problem in a way that would never really happen in a big city.

By the time the air ambulance arrived the man had regained consciousness and the woman had been reunited with her family. Jenna listened as Ryan exchanged information with the paramedics and masterminded the man's transfer. As the helicopter lifted off for the short trip to the mainland, she turned to him.

His face was tanned from the sun and the wind, his dark hair a surprising contrast to his ice-blue eyes.

Trapped by his gaze, Jenna stood still, inexplicably drawn to him. She forgot about the small stones pressing into her bare feet; she forgot that she was confused about her feelings. She forgot everything except the astonishing bolt of chemistry that pulled her towards Ryan.

She wanted to kiss him again.

She wanted to kiss him now.

Feeling like a teenager on her first date, she leaned towards him, melting like chocolate on a hot day. His hands came down on her shoulders and she heard the harshness of his breathing.

Yes, now, she thought dreamily, feeling the strength of his fingers—

'Mum!'

The voice of a real teenager carried across the beach, and Jenna jumped as if she'd been shot as she recognised Lexi's appalled tones. For a moment she stared into Ryan's eyes, and then she turned her head and saw her daughter staring at her in undisguised horror.

'What are you doing?'

Her heart pounding and her mouth dry, Jenna was grateful for the distance, which ensured that at least her daughter couldn't see her scarlet cheeks.

What *was* she doing?

She was a divorced mother of thirty-three and she'd been on the verge of kissing a man with virtually all the islanders watching.

'We probably ought to get back to the barbecue...' Ryan's tone was level and she nodded, feeling numb.

'Yes. Absolutely.' If Lexi hadn't shouted she would have put her arms around his neck and kissed him.

And what would that have done for her relationship with her daughter, let alone her relationship with Ryan?

This was her new life and she'd almost blown it. If Lexi hadn't called out to her she would have risked everything. And all for what? A kiss?

'If they've eaten all the food, I'll kill someone.' Apparently suffering none of her torment, Ryan turned towards the steps that led down to the sand, as relaxed as if they'd been having a conversation about the weather. 'How are things, Jim?'

Jim?

It took Jenna a moment to realise that the ferryman was standing by the steps, chatting to another islander. Had he been that close all the time? There could have been a fire, a flood and a hurricane, and all she would have noticed was Ryan.

'Another life saved, Doc.' Grinning, Jim scratched the back of his neck and looked up at the sky, where the helicopter was now no more than a tiny dot. 'Another good holiday experience on Glenmore. They'll be coming back. I overheard someone saying on the ferry this morning that they'd booked a short break here just so that they could ask a doctor about a skin rash, because you lot always know what you're doing.'

Ryan rolled his eyes. 'I'll mention it to Logan. We obviously need to make more of an effort to be useless.'

Jenna produced a smile, pretending to listen, wondering whether she could just slink onto the ferry and take the first sailing back to the mainland in the morning. Maybe distance would make her forget the kiss, because nothing else was working—not even an emergency.

Lexi was waiting for them at the bottom of the steps. 'Mum? What were you doing?'

'She was debriefing with Dr McKinley,' Evanna said smoothly, and Jenna jumped with shock because she hadn't seen Evanna standing next to her daughter. Last time she'd looked Evanna had been serving sausages and salad. But somehow the other woman had materialised at the foot of the steps, Charlie in her arms. 'I gather everything went smoothly, Jenna? Rapid response from the air ambulance? Did things go according to plan?'

Grateful as she was for Evanna's focus on the professional, Jenna didn't manage to respond.

Fortunately Ryan took over. 'Things don't always go according to plan,' he said softly, 'but that's life, isn't it? Ideally I would have liked to lose the audience, but you can't choose where these things happen.'

Jenna couldn't work out whether he was talking about the medical emergency or the fact she'd almost kissed him. They'd had an audience for both. and she was painfully aware that she'd embarrassed him as much as herself. These were his friends. His colleagues. No doubt he'd be on the receiving end of suggestive remarks for the rest of the summer. Yes, he'd kissed her on the beach, but that had been early in the morning with no one watching.

Because Lexi was still looking at her suspiciously, Jenna forced herself to join in the discussion. 'I—it was a bit unexpected. I'm not used to dealing with emergencies.' And she wasn't used to being attracted to a man. She'd behaved like a crazed, desperate woman.

'From what I've heard you were fantastic—a real Glenmore nurse.' Evanna was generous with her praise. 'We're expected to be able to turn our hands to pretty much anything. People are already singing your praises all over the island.' She tucked her hand through Jenna's arm, leading her back across the beach as if they'd been friends for ever. 'Word travels fast in this place. How are your feet?'

Jenna glanced down and realised that she'd forgotten she wasn't wearing shoes. 'Sore. I need to find my sandals.' Her face was burning and she didn't dare look round to see where Ryan was. Hiding, probably—afraid of the desperate divorcee who had tried to attack him. As for Lexi, she still wasn't smiling, but the scowl had left her features. Which presumably meant that Evanna's explanation had satisfied her.

'Your Lexi is so brilliant with the children.' Evanna led her back to the food and heaped potato salad on a plate. 'Logan— find something delicious for Jenna. She's earned it.'

Jenna accepted the food, even though the last thing she felt like was eating. She just wanted to go home and work out what she was going to say to Ryan next time she saw him on his own.

She had to apologise. She had to explain that she had absolutely no idea what had happened to her. Yes, she'd got a dog, she ate fish three times a week and she'd drunk beer from a bottle, but kissing a man in public…

Lexi flicked her hair away from her face. 'I'm off to play volleyball.' With a final glance in her direction, her daughter sauntered off across the sand towards Fraser, who was laughing with a friend, a can of cola in his hand. 'See you later.'

Jenna wanted to leave, but she knew that would draw attention to herself, and she'd already attracted far too much attention for one evening. Even without turning her head she was painfully aware of Ryan talking to Logan, discussing the air ambulance.

She wondered whether she should request that the air ambulance come back for her when they'd finished. She felt as though she needed it.

'Have a drink.' Clearly reading her mind, Evanna pushed a large glass of wine into her hand. 'And don't look so worried. Everything is fine. You and Ryan were a great team.'

Jenna managed a smile, but all she could think was, *Why am I feeling like this?*

She had to forget him. She had to forget that kiss.

Thank goodness tomorrow was Sunday and she didn't have to work. She had a whole day to talk some sense into herself.

CHAPTER SEVEN

10 reasons why I shouldn't fall in love with Ryan:
    I've been divorced less than a year
    I am too old
    I'm ordinary and he is a sex god
    Being with him puts me off my food
    I have Lexi to think of
    I need to act my age
    I have to work with the man
    He'll hurt me
    I'm not his type

'MUM?'

Jenna dropped the pen before number ten and flipped the envelope over. 'I'm in the kitchen. You're up early.' Too early. Deciding that she couldn't hide the envelope without looking suspicious, Jenna slammed her mug of tea on it and smiled brightly. 'I was expecting you to sleep in.'

'I was hungry, and anyway I'm meeting the gang.' Yawning, Lexi tipped cereal into a bowl and added milk. 'You're up early, too.'

'I had things to do.' Like making a list of reasons why she shouldn't be thinking of Ryan.

Her head throbbing and her eyelids burning from lack of

sleep, Jenna stood up and filled the kettle, bracing herself for the awkward questions she'd been dreading all night. 'You normally want to lie in bed.'

'That's only during term time, when there's nothing to get up for except boring old school.' Lexi frowned at her and then eyed the mug on the envelope. 'Why are you making tea when you haven't drunk the last one?'

Jenna stared in horror at the mug on the table.

Because she wasn't concentrating.

She'd been thinking about the kiss again.

Exasperated with herself, she picked up the half-full mug and scrunched the envelope in her hand. 'This one is nearly cold. And anyway, I thought you might like one.'

Lexi gaped at her. 'I don't drink tea. And why are you hiding that envelope? Is it a letter from Dad or something?'

'It's nothing—I mean—' Jenna stammered. 'I wrote a phone number on it—for a plumber—that tap is still leaking—'

Lexi's eyes drifted to the tap, which stubbornly refused to emit even a drop of water. 'So if there's a number on it, why did you just scrunch it up?'

'I only remembered about the number after I scrunched it up.'

Lexi shrugged, as if her mother's strange behaviour was so unfathomable it didn't bear thinking about. 'I won't be back for lunch. I'm meeting Fraser and a bunch of his friends up at the castle ruins at nine. We're making a day of it.'

'It's Sunday. Archaeology club isn't until tomorrow.'

'Not officially, but the chief archaeologist guy is going to show us the dungeons and stuff. Really cool.'

'Oh.' Still clutching the envelope, Jenna sat back down at the table, relieved that there wasn't going to be an inquisition about the night before. 'I was going to suggest we made a picnic and went for a walk on the cliffs, but if you're meeting your friends—well, that's great.'

Lexi pushed her bowl away and stood up. 'Do I look OK?'

Jenna scanned the pretty strap top vacantly, thinking that the blue reminded her of Ryan's eyes in the seconds before he'd kissed her on the beach. Had she ever felt this way about Clive? Was it just that she'd forgotten? And how did Ryan feel about her?

'Mum? What do you think?'

'I think he's a grown man and he knows what he's doing.'

'What?' Lexi stared at her. 'He's fifteen. Same age as me.'

Jenna turned scarlet. 'That's what I mean. He's almost a man. And I'm sure he's responsible.'

'But I didn't ask you—' Lexi shook her head in frustration. 'What *is* wrong with you this morning? Mum, are you OK?'

No, Jenna thought weakly. She definitely wasn't. 'Of course I'm OK. Why wouldn't I be? I'm great. Fine. I'm good. Really happy. Looking forward to a day off.'

Lexi backed away, hands raised. 'All right, all right. No need to go overboard—I was just asking. You look like you're having a breakdown or something.'

'No. No breakdown.' Her voice high pitched, Jenna pinned a smile on her face. She was good at this bit. Feel one emotion, show another. She'd done it repeatedly after her marriage had fallen apart. Misery on the inside, smile on the outside. Only in this case it was crazy lust-filled woman on the inside, respectable mother on the outside. 'Have a really, really nice day, Lexi. I'm glad you've made friends so quickly.'

Lexi narrowed her eyes suspiciously. 'What? No lecture? No "Don't go too near the edge or speak to strangers"? No "Sex is for two people who love each other and are old enough to understand the commitment"? Are you sure you're OK?'

Back to thinking about Ryan, Jenna barely heard her. 'I thought you wanted me to worry less.'

'Yes, but I didn't exactly expect you to manage it!'

'Well, you can relax. I haven't actually stopped worrying— I've just stopped talking about it.' Still clutching the envelope,

Jenna stood up and made herself another cup of tea. 'I've brought you up with the right values—it's time I trusted you. Time I gave you more independence and freedom to make your own mistakes.'

'Mum, are you feeling all right?'

No. No, she wasn't feeling all right.

She was feeling very confused. She was thinking about nothing but sex and that just wasn't her, was it? Had Clive's brutal betrayal left her so wounded and insecure that she needed affirmation that she was still an attractive woman? Or was it something to do with wanting what you couldn't have?

Lexi folded her arms. 'So you're perfectly OK if I just spend the day up at the castle, taking drugs and making out with Fraser?'

'That's fine.' Thinking of the way Ryan's body had felt against hers, Jenna stared blindly out of the kitchen window. 'Have a nice time.'

'OK, this is spooky. I just told you I'm going to use drugs and make out and you want me to have a *nice time*?'

Had she really said that? 'I know you wouldn't do that.' Jenna mindlessly tidied the kitchen. 'You're too sensible. You're always telling me you're going to have a career before children.'

'Sex doesn't have to end in children, Mum.' Lexi's voice was dry as she picked up her phone and her iPod and walked towards the door. 'One day, when you're old enough, I'll explain it all to you. In the meantime I'll leave you to your incoherent ramblings. Oh, and you might want to remove the teabags from the washing machine—you'll be looking for them later.'

She'd put the teabags in the washing machine?

Jenna extracted them, her cheeks pink, her brain too fuddled to form an appropriate response. 'Have fun. Don't forget your key.'

'You're acting so weird.' Lexi slipped it into her pocket, staring at her mother as if she were an alien. 'You know—last night, for a moment, I really thought—'

Jenna's breathing stopped. 'What did you think?'

'I thought that you—' Lexi broke off and shrugged. 'Never mind. Crazy idea, and anyway I was wrong. Thank goodness. What are you planning to do today?'

Chew over everything that had happened the night before; try not to spend the day thinking of Ryan; remind herself that she was too old to have crushes on men— 'Housework,' Jenna muttered, staring blindly at the pile of unwashed plates that were waiting to be stacked in the dishwasher. 'Catch up on a few things. The laundry basket is overflowing, and I need to weed the herbaceous border.' It all sounded like a boring day to her, but her answer seemed to satisfy Lexi.

Clearly Lexi had been reassured by Evanna's assertion that the two of them had been discussing the emergency they'd dealt with. Either that or she'd just decided that no man was ever going to be seriously interested in her mother.

'I'll see you later, then. Do you mind if I take Rebel?' Grabbing his lead, Lexi whistled to the dog and sauntered off to meet Fraser and his friends at the castle, leaving Jenna to face a day on her own with her thoughts.

And her thoughts didn't make good company.

Tormented by the memory of what had happened the night before, she pulled out one of the kitchen chairs and sat down with a thump. Then she smoothed the crumpled envelope she'd been clutching and stared at her list. She'd started with ten but there were probably a million reasons why it was a bad idea to kiss Ryan McKinley.

With a groan, she buried her face in her hands. She had to stop this nonsense. She had to pull herself together and act like an adult. She was a mother, for goodness' sake.

'You're obviously feeling as frustrated as I am.' His voice came from the doorway and Jenna flew to her feet, the chair crashing backwards onto the tiled floor, her heart pounding.

'Ryan!' The fact that she'd been thinking about him made the whole thing even more embarrassing—but not as humiliating as the fact that she was wearing nothing but her knickers and the old tee shirt of Lexi's that she'd worn to bed. Jenna tugged at the hem, until she realised that just exposed more of her breasts. 'What are you doing here?'

'Trying to have five minutes with you without the whole of Glenmore watching.' He strode across the kitchen, righting the chair that she'd tipped over. Then he gave her a wicked smile. 'Nice outfit.'

Too shocked to move, Jenna watched him walk towards her, dealing with the fact that a man was looking at her with undisguised sexual interest and he wasn't Clive. There was no mixing this man up with Clive. Her ex-husband was slight of build, with pale skin from spending most of his day in an office. Ryan was tall and broad-shouldered, his skin bronzed from the combination of wind and sun. When she'd looked at Clive she hadn't thought of sex and sin, but when she looked at Ryan—

He stopped in front of her. 'You have fantastic legs.'

A thrill of dangerous pleasure mingled with embarrassment. 'How did you get in?'

'The usual way—through the door.' Before she could say a word, he caught the front of her tee shirt in his hand, jerked her against him and brought his mouth down on hers. A thousand volts of pure sexual chemistry shot through her body and thoughts of sex and sin exploded into reality.

Jenna gripped his arms, feeling hard male muscle flex under her fingers. 'I've been thinking about you—'

'Good. I'd hate to be the only one suffering. You taste so good…' Groaning the words against her lips, Ryan sank his hands into her hair and devoured her mouth as if she were a feast and he was starving. His kiss was hot and hungry, and she felt her knees weaken and her heart pound. Flames licked through her veins and Jenna tightened her grip on his arms, grateful that she was leaning against the work surface.

Engulfed by an explosion of raw need Jenna wrapped her arms around his neck and pressed closer. His hands came round her back and he hauled her against him, leaving her in no doubt as to the effect she had on him. Feeling the hard ridge of his erection, Jenna felt excitement shoot through her body.

Dizzy and disorientated, she moaned against his mouth and he slid his hands under the tee shirt, his fingers warm against her flesh. She gasped as those same fingers dragged over her breasts, moaned as he toyed and teased. And still he kissed her. Mouth to mouth they stood, the skilled sweep of his tongue driving her wild, until she squirmed against him, the ache deep inside her almost intolerable.

Dimly, she heard him groan her name, and then he was lifting her tee shirt over her head and his mouth was on her bare breast. Jenna opened her mouth to tell him that it felt good, but the only sound that emerged was a faint moan, and her breathing became shallow as he drew the sensitive tip into his mouth. Her fingers sank into his thick dark hair as the excitement built, and suddenly she was aware of nothing but the heavy throb in her body and the desperate need for more. Every thought was driven from her mind, but one—

She wanted him. She wanted sex with him, and she didn't care about the consequences.

His mouth was back on hers, the slide of his tongue intimate and erotic.

Shaking now, Jenna reached for the waistband of his jeans and felt his abdomen clench against her fingers. She fumbled ineptly for a few moments, and then his hand closed around her wrist.

'Wait—God, I can't believe the way you make me feel.'

She moaned and pressed her mouth back to his, their breath mingling. 'I want to—'

With obvious difficulty he dragged his mouth from hers. 'I know you do, and so do I, but this time I really don't want to be disturbed—how long is Lexi out for? Is she going to be back in the next few hours?'

'Lexi?' Disorientated, Jenna stared at him for a moment, and then shook her head and rubbed her fingers over her forehead, trying to switch off the response of her body so that she could think clearly. 'Lexi.' She felt as though her personality had been split down the middle—mother and woman. 'She's out, but— What on earth am I doing?' Realising that she was virtually naked, Jenna quickly retrieved her tee shirt from the floor, but she was shaking so much that she couldn't turn it the right way round.

'I wish I hadn't said anything.' His tone rough, Ryan removed it gently from her hands, turned it the right way round and pulled it carefully over her head. 'I just didn't want her walking in on us.'

'No. And it's ridiculous. This whole thing is ridiculous— I'm— And you're—'

He raised an eyebrow. 'Is there any chance of you actually finishing a sentence, because I have no idea what you're thinking.'

'I'm thinking that this is crazy.' Jenna straightened the tee shirt and flipped her hair free. 'I'm thinking that I don't do things like this.'

'That doesn't mean you can't. You hadn't owned a dog or eaten fish until a month ago.'

She gave a hysterical laugh. 'Having sex is slightly different to getting a dog or eating fish.'

'I should hope so. If a few hours in my bed is on a par with eating fish or getting a dog, I'll give up sex.'

'That would be a terrible waste, because you're obviously very good at it.' Jenna slammed her hand over her mouth and stared at him, appalled. 'I can't believe I just said that.'

But he was laughing, his blue eyes bright with humour. 'I love the way you say what you think.'

'What I think is that I don't know what you're doing here with me.' With an embarrassed laugh, she yanked the tee shirt down, covering herself. 'I'm not some nubile twenty-year-old. I'm a mother and I'm thirty-three…' The words died in her throat as he covered her mouth with his fingers.

'You're incredibly sexy.'

Staring up into his cool blue eyes, Jenna gulped, still coming to terms with the feelings he'd uncovered. He'd had his hands on her, and as for his mouth… An earthquake could have hit and she wouldn't have noticed. In fact, she felt as though an earthquake *had* hit.

Everything about her world had changed and it was hard to keep her balance.

But she had to. She couldn't afford the luxury of acting on impulse. She wasn't a teenager.

Thinking of teenagers made her groan and close her eyes.

'Ryan, what are you doing here?' She jabbed her fingers into her hair, horrified by what could have happened. 'We could have— Lexi might have—'

'I saw her leave. And before you panic, no, she didn't see me. I stayed out of the way until she'd disappeared over the horizon. Given the way she guards you, I thought it was wise. She obviously doesn't see her mother as a living, breathing sexual woman.'

'That's because I'm not. I'm not like this. This isn't me.'

'Maybe it *is* you.' His eyes lingered on her mouth. 'Do you want to find out?'

Her heart bumped hard. 'I can't. I have responsibilities.'

'Talking of which, did she give you a hard time about last night?'

'She started to say something and then decided that she'd imagined it all. Thanks to Evanna. But—I'm sorry about last night. I was going to apologise to you.'

'Don't.' His mouth was so close to hers that it was impossible to concentrate.

'You must be furious with me for embarrassing you in public—'

His hand was buried in her hair, his lips moving along her jaw. 'Do I seem furious?' His mouth was warm and clever, and Jenna felt her will-power strained to the limit.

She put a hand on his chest, trying to be sensible. Trying to ignore the way he made her feel.

Then he paused and stooped to retrieve something from the floor. It was her envelope. He would have discarded it had she not given an anguished squeak and reached for it.

'That's mine.'

'What is it?'

'It's nothing.' Jenna snatched at it but he held it out of reach, unfurling it with one hand.

'If it's nothing, why are you trying to stop me reading it?' He squinted at the crumpled paper. '"10 reasons why I shouldn't fall in love with Ryan—" Ah.'

With a groan, Jenna covered her face with her hands. 'Please, just ignore it—'

'No.' His voice was calm and steady. 'If you can make a list of ten reasons not to fall in love with me, I have a right to know what they are.' He scanned the list and frowned. 'I put you off your food? That's why you don't eat?'

Mortified, Jenna just shook her head, and he sighed and tucked the mangled envelope into the back pocket of his jeans.

'If you want my opinion, I don't think it matters that you've been divorced for less than a year, nor do I think your age has any relevance. The fact that I put you off your food might be a problem in the long term, but we won't worry for now. As for Lexi—' He stroked his fingers through her hair. 'I can see that might be a problem. That's why I stopped when I did. I didn't want her to walk in.'

'So you're not just a sex god.' She made a joke of it. 'You're thoughtful, too.'

'For selfish reasons. I want you, and you come with a daughter.'

Did he mean he *wanted her* body or he wanted her? She was afraid to ask and she found it hard to believe that he wanted her at all. 'Why do I always meet you looking my worst?' Jenna couldn't believe the unfairness of it all. He looked like a living, breathing fantasy and she was wearing Lexi's cast off tee shirt.

'I think you look fantastic.' Ryan slid his hand into her hair, studying each tangled curl in detail. 'Does your hair curl naturally?'

'Yes, of course. Do you think I'd pay to make it look like this?' She snapped the words, embarrassed that she was looking her worst when he was looking his best, and really, really confused by the way he made her feel.

'I really like it.' His smile was slow and sexy. 'You look as though you've had a really crazy night in some very lucky man's bed.'

Jenna couldn't concentrate. His fingers were massaging her scalp and she felt his touch right through her body. How did he know how to do that? Her eyes drifted shut and suddenly the impact on her other senses was magnified.

'As a matter of interest, what did you wear to bed when you were married?'

Jenna gulped. 'A long silky nightdress that Clive's mother bought me for Christmas. Why do you want to know?'

'Because I suspect this is another of your little rebellions. And now we've established that Lexi isn't coming back in the immediate future…' His voice husky, Ryan slid his hands under the offending tee shirt and she gasped because his hands were warm and strong and her nerve-endings were on fire.

'Ryan—'

His fingers slid down her back with a slow, deliberate movement that was unmistakably seductive. 'I hate to be the one to point this out, but I have a strong suspicion that neither Clive nor his mother would approve of your current choice of nightwear.'

'They'd be horrified—'

'Which is why you're wearing it.'

Jenna gave a choked laugh. 'Maybe. In which case I'm seriously disturbed and you should avoid me.'

Ryan lifted her chin so that she had no choice but to look at him. 'Is that what you want?'

All the pent-up emotion inside her exploded, as if the gates holding everything back had suddenly been opened. 'No, that isn't what I want! Of course it isn't. But I feel guilty, because I know I shouldn't be doing this, and confused because I've never lost control like that before. I'm angry with myself for being weak-willed, terrified that you'll hurt me—'

'Ah, yes—number eight on your list. Why do you assume I'll hurt you?'

Jenna thought about Clive. If Clive had found her boring, how much more boring would this man find her? 'I'm not very exciting. I'm sure I'm all wrong for you.'

'In what way are you wrong for me?'

'For a start I've never had sex on a desk,' she blurted out, and then paled in disbelief. 'Oh, no—I can't believe I said that—'

'Neither can I. You're saying some really interesting things at the moment.' To give him his due, he didn't laugh. But he did close his hands around her wrists and drew her closer. 'I'm guessing that statement has some significance—am I right?'

Jenna stared at a point on his chest. 'I walked in on them,' she breathed. 'She was lying on his desk.'

'And you think that's what was wrong with your marriage?'

'No. The problems in our marriage went far deeper than that. I wouldn't have wanted to have sex on a desk with Clive, whereas—' She broke off, and he was silent for a moment.

Then he lifted his hand and slowly dragged his finger over her scarlet cheek. 'Whereas you do want to have sex on a desk with me?'

'Yes,' she whispered. 'Well, I don't mean a desk specifically—anywhere… But that's crazy, because I'm just not that sort of person and I know I'm really, really not your type.'

'Number nine on the list. So what *is* my type, Jenna?'

'I don't know. Someone stunning. Young. You're disgustingly handsome and you're sickeningly clever.' She mumbled the words, making a mental note never to commit her thoughts to paper again. 'I may be naive, but I'm not stupid. You could have any woman you want. You don't need to settle for a mess like me. And now you ought to leave, because all I ever do when you're around is embarrass myself. I need to get my head together and think about Lexi.'

'Why do you want to think about Lexi? She's out enjoying herself.'

Jenna felt her heart bump against her chest. 'I don't want to hurt her.'

'Is it going to hurt her if you spend the day with me?' His head was near hers, their mouths still close.

'No. But it might hurt me. I find this whole situation scary,' she confessed softly. 'What if I'm doing this for all the wrong reasons?' She looked up at him. 'What if I'm trying to prove something? What if I'm just using you to prove to myself that someone finds me attractive?'

'That objection wasn't on your list.' His mouth was against her neck, his tongue trailing across the base of her throat. 'You're not allowed to think up new ones.'

'I can't think properly when you do that—'

'Sorry.' But he didn't sound sorry, and he didn't stop what he was doing.

Jenna felt her insides melt but her brain refused to shut up. 'What if I'm just doing this because I'm angry with Clive?'

With a sigh, Ryan lifted his head. 'You're suggesting that kissing me is an act of revenge?'

'I don't know. I have no idea what's going on in my head. What I'm thinking is changing by the minute.'

There was a trace of humour in his eyes as he scanned her face. 'When you kissed me were you thinking of Clive?'

'No! But that doesn't mean it isn't a reasonable theory.'

'Answer me one question.' His mouth was against her neck again and Jenna closed her eyes.

'What?'

'If Lexi wasn't part of the equation—if it were just you and me—what would you like to do now?'

'Spend the day together, as you suggested. But somewhere private. Somewhere no one will see us.' She sighed. 'An impossible request on Glenmore, I know.'

'Maybe not.' Stroking her hair away from her face, Ryan gave a slow smile. 'In fact, I think I know just the place.'

The lighthouse was perched on a circle of grass, and the only approach was down a narrow path that curved out of sight of the road.

'It's the most secluded property on the island.' Ryan held out his hand as she negotiated the stony path. 'Even Mrs Parker has never been down here.'

Jenna shaded her eyes and stared up towards the top of the lighthouse. 'It's incredible. I can't believe it's a house.'

'It used to be fairly basic, but I made a few changes.' Ryan opened the door and she walked through, into a beautiful circular kitchen.

'Oh, my!' Stunned, she glanced around her. It was stylish and yet comfortable, with a huge range cooker, an American fridge and a central island for preparing food. By the window overlooking the sea the owner had placed a table, ensuring that anyone eating there could enjoy the fantastic view. 'A few changes?'

'Quite a few changes.' Ryan leaned against the doorframe, watching her reaction. 'Do you like it?'

'I love it. I had no idea—from the outside it looks…' Lost for words, she shook her head. 'It's idyllic.'

'Do you want breakfast now, or after you've looked round?'

'After…'

'Oh, yes—objection number four.' He gave a faint smile and urged her towards an arched doorway and a spiral staircase. 'I put you off your food. I don't suppose you'd like to tell me why? I don't think I've ever made a woman feel sick before.'

She giggled. 'You don't make me feel sick. You make me sort of churny in my stomach.'

'Sort of churny?' He lifted an eyebrow at her description. 'Is that good or bad?'

'Good, if you're trying to lose weight.'

'Don't. I like you the way you are.' He was right behind her on the stairs and it was impossible not to be aware that it was just the two of them in the house.

'So no one overlooks this?'

'It's a very inhospitable part of the coast of Glenmore—hence the reason they built a lighthouse here originally. This is the living room.'

Jenna emerged into another large, circular room, with high ceilings and glass walls. It had been decorated to reflect its coastal surroundings, with white wooden floors, seagrass matting and deep white sofas. Touches of blue added colour and elegant pieces of driftwood added style. A wood-burning stove stood in the centre of the room. 'This is the most beautiful room I've ever seen. I can't imagine what it must be like to actually live somewhere as special as this.'

'It was virtually a shell when I bought it from the original owner.' Ryan strolled over to the window, his back to her. 'It took me a year to make it properly habitable.'

'Where did you live while you were renovating it?'

'I lived here. Amidst the rubble.'

'You did most of it yourself?'

'All of it except the glazing. I used a lot of glass and it was too heavy for one person to manipulate.'

Stunned, she looked around her. 'You did the building— the plumbing, electricity?'

'I'm a doctor,' he drawled. 'I'm used to connecting pipes and electrical circuits. Building a wall isn't so different to realigning a broken bone—basically you need the thing straight.'

Jenna shook her head in silent admiration and carried on up the spiral staircase. She pushed open a door and discovered a luxurious bathroom, complete with drench shower. Another door revealed a small guest bedroom. Deciding that she'd never seen a more perfect property in her life, Jenna took the final turn in the staircase and found herself in paradise.

The master bedroom had been designed to take maximum advantage of the incredible view, with acres of glass giving a three-hundred-and-sixty-degree outlook on Glenmore.

Speechless, Jenna walked slowly around the perimeter of the breathtaking room. Out of the corner of her eye she was conscious of the enormous bed, but she was also acutely conscious of Ryan, watching her from the head of the spiral staircase. The intimacy was unfamiliar and exciting.

Hardly able to breathe, she stared out across the sparkling sea, watching as the view changed with every step. Far beneath her were vicious rocks that must have sent so many boats tumbling to the bottom of the ocean, but a few paces on and she had a perfect view of the coast path, winding like a ribbon along the grassy flanks of the island. A few more steps and she was looking inland, across wild moorland shaded purple with heather.

'It's like living outside.'

'That was the idea.'

'I can see everything,' she whispered, 'except people. No people.'

'Just beyond the headland is the Scott farm.' Ryan was directly behind her now, and he closed his hands over her shoulders, pointing her in the right direction. 'But everything here is protected land. No building. No people. Occasionally you see someone on the coast path in the distance, but they can't get down here because the rocks are too dangerous. The path we took is the only way down.'

'I've never been anywhere so perfect.' Acutely aware of his touch, Jenna could hardly breathe. He was standing close to her and she could feel the brush of his hard body against hers. Her heart racing, she stared up at the roof—and discovered more curving glass. 'It must be wild here when there's a storm. Is it scary?'

'It's tough glass. You'd be surprised how much sound it blocks out. Do you find storms scary?' He turned her gently, and suddenly she thought that what she was starting to feel for him was far scarier than any storm.

'I don't know.' Looking into his eyes, she felt as though everything in her life was changing. And not only did she not trust her feelings, she knew she couldn't have them. She had to think about Lexi. But Lexi wasn't here now, was she? Maybe there was no future, but there could be a present. She was a woman as well as a mother.

His mouth was close to hers but he didn't kiss her, and she wondered whether he was waiting for her to make the decision.

Jenna lifted her hand to his face, the breath trapped in her throat. His jaw was rough against her fingers and she felt him tense, but still he didn't kiss her. Still he waited.

Consumed by the thrill of anticipation, she wrapped her arms around his neck and lifted her mouth to his, feeling her stomach swoop. It was like jumping off a cliff. As decisions went, this was a big one, and deep down in her gut she knew there would be a price to pay, but right now she didn't care. If she had to pay, she'd pay.

As her lips touched his she felt the ripple of tension spread across his shoulders—felt the coiled power in his athletic frame.

'Be sure, Jenna…' He breathed the words against her mouth, his hand light on her back, still giving her the option of retreat.

But the last thing she had in mind was retreat. She kept her mouth on his and he slid his hands into her hair and held her face still, taking all that she offered and more, his kiss demanding and hungry.

Someone groaned—her or him?—and then his arms came around her and he held her hard against him. The feel of his body made her heart race, and Jenna felt her linen skirt slide to the floor, even though she hadn't actually felt him undo it. And suddenly she was acutely aware of him—of the strength of his hands, the roughness of his jeans against the softness of her skin, the hard ridge of his arousal—

'Jenna—I have to—' His hands were full of her, stripping off her skirt, peeling off underwear until she was naked and writhing against him. And her hands were on him, too, on his zip, which refused to co-operate until he covered her hands with his. This time instead of stopping her, he helped her.

Hearts pounding, mouths fused, they fell to the floor, feasting.

'The bed is a metre away—' Ryan had his mouth on her breast and pleasure stabbed hard, stealing her breath. 'We should probably—'

'No—too far.' Terrified he'd stop what he was doing, Jenna clutched at his hair, gasping as she felt his tongue graze her nipple. Sensation shot through her and he teased, nipped and sucked one rigid peak while using his fingers on the other. The burn inside her was almost intolerable. Her hips writhed against the soft rug and she arched in an instinctive attempt to get closer to him. But she wasn't in charge. He was. Maybe there was some pattern to what he was doing, some sequence, but for her it was all a blur of ecstasy.

The words in her head died as his hand slid between her legs.

It had been two years since a man had touched her intimately, and even before that it had never felt like this. Never before had she felt this restless, burning ache.

'Ryan—' The slow, leisurely stroke of his skilled fingers drove her wild. 'Now.'

'I haven't even started…' His voice was husky against her ear, and his fingers slid deeper. Heat flushed across her skin and her breathing grew shallow. Her hand slid down and circled him and she heard him catch his breath.

'On second thoughts—now seems like a good idea…' He slid his hand under her bottom and lifted her, the blunt head of his erection brushing against her thigh.

Trembling with expectation, Jenna curved one thigh over his back and then groaned when he hesitated. 'Please…'

'Forgot something—' His voice hoarse, he eased himself away from her, reached forward and grabbed something from the cupboard by his bed. 'Damn!' He struggled with the packet while he kissed her again.

Jenna was panting against his mouth. 'Just—can you please—?'

'Yeah, I definitely can.' He hauled her under him, dropping his forehead to hers. 'Are you sure?'

'Is that a serious question?' She was breathless—desperate—conscious of the press of his body against hers. 'If you stop now, Ryan McKinley, I swear, I'll punch you.'

His laugh was low and sexy, and her stomach flipped as

she stared into those blue, blue eyes. And then she ceased to notice anything because the roughness of his thigh brushed against hers and then he was against her and inside her and Jenna decided that if sex had ever felt like this before then she must have lost her memory.

Heat spread through her body and she tried to tell him how good it felt, but the sleek thrust of his body drove thought from her brain. He kissed her mouth, then her neck, ran his hand down her side and under her bottom—lifted her—

She moaned his name and he brought his lips back to hers, taking her mouth even as he took her body, and the pleasure was so intense that she could hardly breathe. Her nails sank into his back and the excitement inside her roared forward like a train with no brakes—

'Oh— I—' Her orgasm consumed her in a flash of brilliant light and exquisite sensation and she heard him growl deep in his throat, surging deeper inside her as she pulsed around him. She sobbed his name, tightened her grip and felt him thrust hard for the last time. They clung, breathless, riding the wave, going where the pleasure took them.

With a harsh groan Ryan dropped his head onto her shoulder, his breathing dragging in his throat. 'Are you OK?'

'No, I don't think so.' Weak and shaky, Jenna stared up at the ceiling, shell shocked, stunned by the intensity of what they'd shared. 'It's never been like that before.'

'That's probably because you've never made love on a wooden floor.' Wincing slightly, Ryan eased his weight off her and rolled onto his back, his arms still round her. 'I need to buy a different floor covering. This was designed for walking on and aesthetic appearance, not for sex. Do you want to move to the bed?'

'I don't want to move at all.' She just wanted to lie here, with him, staring up at the blue sky and the clouds above them. It seemed a fitting view. 'It's perfect here.'

'Perfect, apart from the bruises.'

'I don't have bruises, and even if I do I don't care.' She turned and rested her cheek on his chest, revelling in the opportunity to touch him. 'This morning I was wondering whether I ought to kiss you again—'

'And what did you decide?'

'You interrupted me before I'd made my decision.'

'If you want my opinion, I think you should definitely kiss me again.' His eyes gleamed with humour and he lifted her chin with his fingers and kissed her lightly. 'And again.'

Jenna shifted until she lay on top of him. 'I've never done this before.'

He raised an eyebrow. 'You have a child.'

'I mean I've never been so desperate to have sex I couldn't make it as far as the bed—never lost control like that.' She kissed the corner of his mouth, unable to resist touching him. 'I've never wanted anyone the way I want you. Ever since I arrived on the island I've wanted you. I thought I was going crazy—'

'I was going crazy, too.' He sank his hands into her hair and kissed her. 'Believe me, you're not the only one who has been exercising will-power.'

'I wasn't sure this was what you wanted.' She was conscious that she still knew next to nothing about him, and suddenly a stab of anxiety pierced her happiness. 'Can I ask you something?' Through the open window she could hear the crash of the waves and the shriek of the seagulls, reminding her how isolated they were.

'Yes.'

'Are you married?'

He stilled. 'You think I'd be lying here with you like this if I were married?'

'I don't know. I hope not.'

'And I hope you know me better than that.'

'Now I've made you angry.' Suddenly she wished she

hadn't ruined the mood by asking the question. 'I'm sorry—
I shouldn't have—' She broke off and then frowned, knowing
that her question was a valid one. 'You have to understand that
I thought I knew Clive, and it turned out I didn't.'

'Jenna, I'm not angry. You don't have to talk about this.'

'Yes, I do. You thought it was an unjust question, but to me
it wasn't unjust and I need you to understand that.' Her voice
was firm. 'I lived with a man for sixteen years and I thought
I knew him. I married him and had his child, I slept in his
bed—we made a life together. And it turned out he had a
whole other life going on that didn't involve me. He had three
affairs over the course of our marriage, one of them with a
friend of mine. I didn't find out until the third.'

Ryan pulled her back down into the circle of his arms. 'You
have a right to ask me anything you want to ask me. And I'm
not married. Not any more.'

'Oh.' Digesting that, she relaxed against him, trailing her
fingers over his chest, lingering on dark hair and hard muscle.
'So it went wrong for you, too?'

'Yes.'

She waited for him to say something more but he didn't,
and she lay for a moment, listening to his heartbeat, her fingers on his chest.

Obviously that was why he'd come here, she thought to
herself. Like her, he'd found comfort in doing something,
found a channel for his anger. He'd built something new.

Ryan sighed. 'I'm sure there are questions you want to ask
me.'

But he didn't want to answer them; she knew that.

'Yes, I have a question.' She shifted on top of him, feeling
his instant response. 'How comfortable is that bed of yours?'

'Fruit, rolls, coffee—' Ryan started loading a tray. 'How
hungry are you?'

'Not very. You put me off my food, remember?' Having

pulled on her linen skirt and tee shirt, Jenna sat on a stool watching him.

'You just used up about ten thousand calories. You need to eat.' Ryan warmed rolls in the oven, sliced melon and made a pot of coffee. 'This should be lunch rather than breakfast, but never mind.'

'Lunch? But we—' Her gaze slid to the clock on the wall and her eyes widened. 'Two o'clock?'

'Like I said—ten thousand calories.' And ten thousand volts to his system. He couldn't believe he wanted her again so quickly, but he could happily have taken her straight back to bed.

Ryan grabbed butter and a jar of thick golden honey and then handed her some plates and mugs. 'You can carry these. I'll bring the rest.'

She stood still, holding the plates and mugs, staring at him.

Removing the rolls from the oven, he glanced at her. 'What's wrong?'

'Nothing.' Her voice was husky, and he frowned as he tipped the warm bread into a basket.

'Honesty, Jenna, remember?'

'It feels strange,' she admitted, 'being here with you like this.'

'Strange in a good way or strange in a bad way?'

'In a scary way. I was with Clive for sixteen years and he was my only boyfriend.'

Thinking about it, he realised he'd probably known that all along, but hearing it was still a shock. 'Your only boyfriend?'

'I met him when I was sixteen. I had Lexi when I was eighteen.'

Ryan wondered whether her selfish ex-husband had taken advantage of her. 'Does that have anything to do with why you have a difficult relationship with your mother?'

'I've always disappointed her.'

He frowned. 'I can't imagine you disappointing anyone.'

But he could imagine her trying to please everyone, and her next words confirmed it.

'My parents had plans for me—which didn't involve me getting pregnant as a teenager.' Her head dipped and she pulled a pair of sunglasses out of the bag on her lap. 'Are we eating outside? I'll probably need these. It's sunny.'

He remembered the conversation she'd had with her mother. How distressed she'd been. 'So what did they want you to do?'

'Something respectable. I had a place lined up at Cambridge University to read English—my parents liked to boast about that. They were bitterly upset when I gave it up.'

'Did you have to give it up?'

'I chose to. Everyone thought I'd be a terrible mother because I was a teenager, and it made me even more determined to be the best mother I could be. I don't see why teenagers can't be good mothers—I'm not saying it's easy, but parenthood is never easy, whatever age you do it.' Tiny frown lines appeared on her forehead. 'I hate the assumption that just because you're young, you're going to be a dreadful parent. I know plenty of bad parents who waited until their thirties to have children.'

Ryan wondered if she was referring to her own. 'For what it's worth, I think you're an amazing mother.'

'Thank you.' Her voice was husky as she cleaned her sunglasses with the edge of her tee shirt. 'I don't think I'm amazing, but I love Lexi for who she is, not what she does. And I've always let her know that.'

'Who she is, not what she does…' Ryan repeated her words quietly, thinking that his own parents could have taken a few lessons from Jenna. In his home, praise had always revolved around achievement.

Jenna fiddled with her glasses. 'My parents were always more interested in what I did than who I was, and I was determined not to be like that. Clive worked—I stayed at home. Traditional, I know, but it was the way I wanted it.'

'Can I ask you something personal? Did you marry him because you loved him or because you were pregnant?'

She hesitated. 'I thought I loved him.'

'And now you're not sure?'

'How can you love someone you don't even know?' Her voice cracked slightly and Ryan crossed the kitchen and dragged her into his arms.

'The guy is clearly deranged.' Dropping a kiss on her hair, he eased her away from him. 'So now I understand why you asked me that question. You must find it impossible to trust another man.'

'No.' She said the word fiercely. 'Clive lied to me, but I know all men aren't like that—just as not all teenage mothers are inept and not all boys wearing hoodies are carrying knives. I won't generalise. I don't trust him, that's true, but I don't want Lexi growing up thinking the whole male race is bad. I won't do that to her.'

Her answer surprised him. He'd met plenty of people with trust issues.

He had a few of his own.

'You're a surprising person, Jenna Richards.' Young in many ways, and yet in others more mature than many people older than her.

'I'm an ordinary person.'

He thought about the way she loved her child, the way she was determined to be as good a mother as she could be. He thought about the fact that she'd been with the same man since she was sixteen. 'There's nothing ordinary about you. I'm intrigued about something, though.' He stroked her hair away from her face, loving the feel of it. 'If you were at home with Lexi, when did you train as a nurse?'

'Once Lexi started school. I had a network of friends—

many of them working mothers. We helped each other out.
Sisterhood. They'd take Lexi for me when I was working, I'd
take their children on my days off. Sometimes I had a house
full of kids.'

He could imagine her with children everywhere. 'Can I ask
you something else? Why didn't you ever have more children?
You obviously love them.'

'Clive didn't want more. He decided Lexi was enough.'

'Like he decided that you weren't going to have a dog
or eat fish?'

She gave a shaky smile. 'Are you suggesting my final act
of rebellion should be to have a baby? I think that might be
taking it a bit far. And anyway, I couldn't do that now.'

'Why not?'

'Well, for a start, I'm too old.'

'You're thirty-three. Plenty of women don't have their first
child until that age.'

She looked at him, and he knew she was wondering why
he was dwelling on the subject. 'And then there's Lexi. If I
had a baby now, it would be difficult for her.'

'Why?'

'Because there have been enough changes in her life. I
suspect that at some point, probably soon, her father is going
to have another child. I don't want to add to the confusion. I
want her relationship with me to be as stable as possible.
Why are you asking?'

Why *was* he asking? Unsettled by his own thoughts, Ryan
turned his attention back to his breakfast. 'I'm just saying
you're not too old to have a child.' He kept his voice even. 'Put
your sunglasses on. You're right about it being sunny outside.'

CHAPTER EIGHT

IT WAS an affair full of snatched moments and secret assignations, all tinged with the bittersweet knowledge that it couldn't possibly last.

At times Jenna felt guilty that she was keeping her relationship with Ryan from Lexi, but her daughter was finally settled and happy and she was afraid to do or say anything that might change that.

She just couldn't give Ryan up.

They'd meet at the lighthouse at lunchtime, make love until they were both exhausted, and then part company and arrive back at the surgery at different times.

And, despite the subterfuge, she'd never been happier in her life.

'I actually feel grateful to Clive,' she murmured one afternoon as they lay on his cliffs, staring at the sea. Her hand was wrapped in his and she felt his warm fingers tighten. 'If he hadn't done what he did, I wouldn't be here now. I wouldn't have known it was possible to feel like this. It's scary, isn't it? You're in a relationship, and you have nothing to compare it to, so you say to yourself this is it. This is how it's supposed to feel. But you always have a sense that something is missing.'

'Did you?'

'Yes, but I assumed it was something in me that was lacking, not in my relationship.'

'Life has a funny way of working itself out.' He turned his head to look at her. 'Have you told Lexi about us yet?'

A grey cloud rolled over her happiness. 'No,' she said. 'Not yet.'

'Are you going to tell her?'

'I don't know.'

'You're afraid of her reaction?'

'Yes. She was devastated when Clive left. Horrified that he was involved with another woman. Apart from the obvious issues, teenagers don't like to see their parents as living, breathing sexual beings.'

And she didn't know what to say. *I've taken a lover...*

What exactly was their relationship? What could there be?

Ryan rolled onto his side and propped himself up on his elbow so that he could see her. 'I want to be with you, Jenna. I want more than lunchtimes and the occasional Sunday afternoon when Lexi is with her friends. I want more.'

Looking into his blue eyes, she felt her heart spin and dance. 'How much more?'

'I love you.' Ryan touched her face gently, as if making a discovery. 'I've loved you since you stepped off that boat looking like someone who had walked away from an accident.'

'You love me?' Jenna was jolted by a burst of happiness and he smiled.

He looked more relaxed than she'd ever seen him. 'Is that a surprise?'

'I didn't dare hope. I thought it might be just—' She was whispering, afraid that she might disturb the dream. 'I love you, too. I've never felt this way about anyone before. I didn't know it was possible.'

'Neither did I.' He kissed her gently, stroked her hair protectively with a hand that wasn't quite steady. Then he gave a shake of his head. 'You've never asked me about my marriage or why I ended up here. I'm sure there are things you want to know about me.'

'I assumed that if there was anything you wanted me to know, you'd tell me when you were ready.'

'You're a very unusual woman, do you know that? You're able to love me, not knowing what went before?'

'It's not relevant to how I feel about you.'

He breathed in deeply, his eyes never shifting from hers. 'I was married—to Connie. She was a very ambitious woman. Connie was born knowing what she wanted in life and nothing was going to stand in her way. We met when we were medical students. We were together briefly, and then met up again when we were both consultants in the same hospital. Looking back on it, we were a disaster waiting to happen, but at the time I suppose it must have seemed right.'

Thinking of her own situation, Jenna nodded. 'That happens.'

His laugh was tight and humourless. 'I think the truth is I was too busy for a relationship and Connie understood that. I was fighting my way to the top and I didn't need a woman asking me what time I'd be home at night. Connie didn't care what time I came home because she was never there to see. She was fighting *her* way to the top, too.'

Jenna sat quietly, letting him speak. She had an image in her head. An image of a beautiful, successful woman. The sort of woman she'd always imagined a man like him would choose. The cream of the crop. Bright and brilliant, like him. They would have been a golden couple. 'Was she beautiful?'

'No.' His hand dropped from her face and he sat up. Stared out across the sea. 'Physically I suppose she would be considered beautiful,' he conceded finally. 'But to me beauty is so much more than sleek hair and well-arranged features. Connie was cold. Selfish. Beauty is who you are and the way you behave. We were both very wrapped up in our careers. We worked all day, wrote research papers in what little spare time we had—our house had two offices.' He frowned and shook his head. 'How could I ever have thought that what we had was a marriage?'

'Go on…'

'I wanted us to start a family.'

'Oh.' It hadn't occurred to her that he might have a child. That was one question she hadn't asked. 'You have—?'

'I brought the subject up one night, about a week after I'd made Consultant. I thought it would be the perfect time.'

'She didn't agree?'

He stared blindly across the ocean and into the far distance. 'She told me she'd been sterilised.'

Jenna sat up. 'She— Oh, my gosh—and you didn't know?' She licked her lips, digesting the enormity of it.

'At medical school she decided she didn't ever want to have a baby. She wanted a career and didn't want children. In her usual ruthlessly efficient way she decided to deal with the problem once and for all. Unfortunately she didn't share that fact with me.' The confession was rough and hoarse, and she knew for sure he hadn't spoken the words to anyone else. Just her. The knowledge that he'd trusted her with something so personal was like a gift, fragile and precious, and Jenna tried to understand how he must be feeling, unwilling to break the connection between them by saying something that might make him regret his show of trust.

In the end she just said what was in her heart. 'That was wrong. Very wrong.'

'Some of the blame was mine. I made assumptions— didn't ask—I suppose I could be accused of being chauvinistic. I presumed we'd do the traditional thing at some point. It came as a shock to discover she had no intention of ever having a family.'

Jenna reached out a hand and touched his shoulder. 'She should have told you.'

'That was my feeling. I suddenly realised I'd been living with a stranger. That I didn't know her at all.' He gave a wry smile. 'But you know how that feels, don't you?'

'Only too well. I was living in this imaginary world—thinking things were fine. But Clive was living a completely different life. A life I didn't even see.' She looped her arms around her legs and rested her chin on her knees. 'I suppose part of the problem was that we just didn't communicate. We fell into marriage because I was pregnant and because it was what my parents expected. I made assumptions about him. He made assumptions about me.' Jenna turned her head and looked at him. 'So you told Connie you wanted a divorce?'

'Yes. I discovered that although I'd achieved what could be considered huge success in my professional life, my personal life was a disaster. I hadn't even thought about what I wanted, and suddenly I realised that what I wanted was the thing I didn't have—someone alongside me who loved me, who wanted to share their life with me. I wanted to come home at night to someone who cared about what sort of day I'd had. I didn't want our only communication to be via voice-mail. And I wanted children. Connie thought I was being ridiculous—her exact words were, "It's not as if you're ever going to change a nappy, Ryan, and I'm certainly not doing it, so why would we want children?"'

'She didn't want a divorce?'

'I was flying high in my career and she liked that. I looked good on her CV.' There was a bitter note to his voice and his eyes were flint-hard. 'Being with me opened doors for her.'

'Did she love you?'

'I have no idea. If she did then it was a very selfish kind of a love. She wanted me for what I added to her, if that makes sense.'

'Yes, it makes sense. I don't know much about relationships…' Jenna thought about her own relationship with Clive '…but I do know that real love is about giving. It's about wanting someone else's happiness more than your own. If you care about someone, you want what's right for them.'

And that was the way she felt about Ryan, she realised. She wanted him to be happy.

Ryan put his arm around her shoulders and drew her against him. 'That's what you do with Lexi, all the time. You're lucky to have her. Lucky to have that bond.'

'Yes.' She melted as he kissed her, knowing that everything was changing. Once again life had taken her in a direction she hadn't anticipated, but this time the future wasn't terrifying. It was exciting. 'I'm going to talk to her. I've decided. I think maybe she's old enough to understand.' Strengthened by her feelings and his, she suddenly felt it was the right thing to do.

'You're going to talk to her about us?'

'Yes. This is what life is, isn't it? It's the happy and the sad and the unpredictable. It would be wrong to pretend anything different. Lexi needs to know that life is sometimes hard and that things can't always stay the same. She needs to know that change isn't always bad and that the unfamiliar can become familiar. And she needs to know that my love for her will never change, no matter what happens to the way we live.'

Ryan stroked his fingers over her cheek. 'You're the most selfless person I've ever met. When your husband walked out, who supported you? Not your mother, I assume. Your friends?'

'For a while. Then I discovered that they'd all known he was having the affair and that they'd known about his other affairs and hadn't told me.' Jenna pulled away from him. 'I found that hard. That and all the advice. "Turn a blind eye." "Dress like a pole dancer and seduce him back—"'

There was amusement in his eyes. 'Did you adopt that suggestion?'

'Of course—I went around wearing nothing but fishnets and a basque.' Pleased that she was able to make a joke about something she'd never thought would seem funny, she wound a strand of hair around her finger. 'To be honest, I didn't want him back. Not after I found out that he'd had a string of affairs throughout our marriage. But the worst thing of all was the way he behaved towards Lexi—it was as if he suddenly just washed his hands of her. His own daughter!' Humour faded and anger flooded through her, fresh as it had been on that first day. 'Whatever he felt about me, that was no excuse for cutting Lexi out of his life.'

'Forget him now.' His voice was rough as he pulled her back to him. 'He was your past. I'm your future.'

Jenna stared at him, silenced by the possibilities that extended in front of her. She wanted to ask what he meant. She wanted to ask whether the future meant a few weeks, or more than that, but she was terrified of voicing the question in case the answer was something she didn't want to hear.

He was watching her, absorbing her reaction. 'Jenna, I know this is soon, but—' There was a buzzing sound from his pocket, and Ryan swore fluently and dragged out his phone. 'Maybe there are some advantages to living in a city—at least someone else can carry the load when you want some time off.' He checked the number and frowned. 'It's Logan. I'd better take this—sorry.'

As he talked to the other doctor, Jenna gently extracted herself from his grip, wondering what he'd been about to say. It was obvious that she wasn't going to find out quickly, because Ryan was digging in his pocket for his car keys as he talked, the expression on his face enough for her to know that the phone call was serious.

He sprang to his feet. 'I'll get up there now.' His eyes flickered to hers. 'And I'll take Jenna with me—no, don't worry, we'll handle it together.'

Realising that she was supposed to help him with some-thing, Jenna stood up and brushed the grass off her skirt.

Ryan was already striding towards the path that led up to his car. 'Have you done any emergency work?'

'Sorry?' Jenna jammed her feet into her shoes and sprinted after him, wondering how the tone of the afternoon could have shifted so quickly.

Glenmore, she thought, and its ever-changing moods.

Even the weather had changed. While they'd been talking the blue sky had turned an ominous grey and the sea a gunmetal-blue.

There was a storm coming.

'Did you ever work in an emergency department?' His mouth grim, Ryan was in the car and firing up the engine be-fore she had time to answer the question.

'Yes. But it was quite a few years ago. What do you need me to do?' Her head smacked lightly against the headrest as he accelerated along the empty road, and Jenna felt the power of the car come to life around her. She felt a shimmer of nerves mingled with anticipation. What if she wasn't up to the job?

To give herself confidence she cast a glance at Ryan, look-ing at his broad shoulders and strong, capable hands. He shifted gears like a racing driver, pushing the car to its limits as he negotiated the tight turns and narrow roads that led from the lighthouse. Even after a comparatively short time she knew he would be able to handle anything he encountered, and that knowledge gave her courage. 'Tell me what's happened.'

'Group of teenagers tombstoning on the Devil's Jaws. It's close to here.'

'Tombstoning?' Jenna rummaged in her pocket and found something to tie back her hair. 'What's that?'

'It's when they stand on the top of a cliff and jump into the sea.' Ryan slowed to take a sharp bend. 'The problem is the depth of the water changes according to the tide. Even when the tide is on your side it's a dangerous activity. And the Devil's Jaws is the most dangerous place you could wish for. It's narrow there—the cliffs have formed a tight channel, so not only can you kill yourself when you hit the bottom, if you get really lucky you can kill yourself on the way down.'

'Kids are doing that? Can't they fence the cliffs off or something?'

'It *is* fenced off. The place is lethal. No one is meant to go within a hundred metres of it, but you know teenagers.' He swung the car into a space at the side of the road and killed the engine. 'We have to walk from here. Are you afraid of heights?'

'I don't know. I don't think so.'

'Watch your footing. To add to the fun, the rocks are crumbling.' Ryan opened his boot and Jenna blinked as she saw the contents.

'You carry ropes in your boot?'

'I climb sometimes.' Without elaborating, he selected several ropes and started piling equipment into a large rucksack. Then he opened his medical bag and added another series of items, including drugs he thought he was going to need. His movements were swift and economical, brutally efficient.

Jenna focused on the drugs. 'Ketamine?'

'I prefer it to morphine. It doesn't produce respiratory depression or hypotension, and in analgesic doses it produces a mild bronchodilator effect.'

'Translate that into English?' A voice came from behind them and Jenna turned to see Nick Hillier, the island policeman. Only today he wasn't smiling.

'It means it controls the pain without affecting the breathing.' Ryan hoisted the bag out of the boot. 'Is it as bad as they say?'

'Worse. Two in the water—one trapped halfway down the cliff. They're right in the Jaws.'

'Of course they are—that's where they get the maximum adrenaline rush.'

'The one stuck on the cliff might be all right, as long as he doesn't let go, but he's getting tired. Coastguard helicopter has chosen today to have a technical problem—they're fixing it, but the cavalry isn't going to be arriving any time soon.' Nick sucked in a breath. 'I don't want anyone going near the edge. I don't want more casualties. We're going to wait and hope to hell they get that helicopter airborne in the next ten minutes. I think this is a rescue best carried out from the air or the sea.'

'I'll take a look at it. Then I'll decide.' Ryan lifted the rucksack onto his back and walked over the grass towards a gate. A sign warned the public that the area was dangerous. Dropping his rucksack onto the other side, Ryan vaulted the gate. Nick climbed over slightly more awkwardly, holding out a hand to Jenna.

She wondered who was going to have the last say on this one. The law or the doctor.

His mind clearly working in the same direction, Nick became visibly stressed. 'Ryan, you know how risky it is. A climber was killed abseiling from here earlier in the summer—the rocks sawed through his rope.'

'Then he didn't have his rope in the right place.' Ryan dropped his rucksack again, onto the grass a safe distance from the edge. 'There are injured kids, Nick. What do you expect me to do? Leave them?'

'My job is to make sure we rescue them with minimum further casualties—that doesn't involve you abseiling down a sheer, crumbling rock face.'

Listening to them, Jenna felt her heart race, and she wondered if she was going to be any use at all.

Yes, she'd worked in an emergency department for a short time, but working in a well-equipped department was quite different from giving pre-hospital care on a sheer cliff face.

She was so busy worrying about her own abilities that it

was a few seconds before she noticed the teenager sitting on the grass. He was shivering and his face was white.

Focusing on his face, Jenna recognised Fraser and her stomach dropped. Suddenly everything seemed to happen in slow motion. She was aware of the guilt in Fraser's anguished glance, and of Ryan turning his head to look at her.

And those looks meant only one thing—

That it was Lexi who was lying in the grip of the Devil's Jaws.

Maternal instinct overwhelming everything else, Jenna gave a low moan of denial and stepped towards the edge, unthinking.

Ryan caught her arm in an iron grip.

'Don't take another step.' His hand was a steadying force and his voice was hard, forcing itself through the blind panic that clouded her thinking. 'Breathe. Up here, you don't run. You take small steps. You look where you're going and you make sure it's safe underfoot. I'll get her. I swear to you I'll get her. But I can't do it if I'm worrying about you going over the edge.'

Jenna stood still, held firm by the strength of his hand and the conviction in his voice.

Fraser struggled to his feet, his lips dry and cracked from the wind and the sun. 'You don't understand—she didn't jump. Lexi was trying to stop Matt doing it—we both were. But he did it anyway—he jumped at the wrong moment. You have to get it exactly right or you hit the rocks.' His voice shook. He was a teenager on the cusp of manhood, but today he was definitely more boy than man. 'Lexi went down there to save Matt. We could see him slipping under the water. He was going to drown. Jamie tried first, but he lost his nerve halfway down and now he can't move. I dunno—he just freaked out or something. So Lexi did it. She insisted. She was dead scared about getting down there, but she said she'd done first aid so she should be the one.'

'She climbed down?' There was a strange note in Ryan's voice and already he had his hands in his rucksack. 'Fraser, take this rope for me.'

'You should have seen her—she was amazing. Just went down slowly, hand and foot, hand and foot, muttering "Three points of contact on the rock face…" or something.'

'She did a climbing course last summer,' Jenna said faintly. Last summer—just before everything had fallen apart. 'It was indoors on a climbing wall in London.'

Nowhere near greasy, slippery rocks or furious boiling sea.

Ryan's gaze met hers for a moment. 'I'd say that was money well spent.'

Fraser was sweating. 'I almost had a heart attack watching her. I'm not good with heights since I fell into that dungeon.' He looked at Jenna, shrinking. 'I'm really sorry. I tried to stop her…'

'It isn't your fault, Fraser.' Jenna's lips were stiff and her heart was pounding. 'Lexi is not your responsibility. She's old enough to make her own decisions.'

'She's as sure-footed as a goat.' There was awe in Fraser's voice. 'Matt was face-down in the water and she dragged him towards the rocks. She's been holding him, but he's too heavy for her to get him out by herself and the tide is coming in. The water level is rising. The ledge they're on will be underwater soon.'

That news made Jenna's knees weaken with panic, but Ryan was icy calm. When he spoke there was no doubt in anyone's mind who was in charge of the rescue.

'Fraser, I want you to stay here and act as runner. Is your mobile working?'

'Yes, the signal is good.'

'Keep it switched on. Dr McNeil is bringing equipment from the surgery. If the helicopter is delayed, then that will change the way we manage Matt's injuries.' Ryan stepped into a harness and adjusted it with hands that were steady and confident. 'Keep the phone line clear—if I need to talk to you, I'll call.'

Nick stepped forward and caught his arm. 'Ryan, for

goodness' sake, man, I'm telling you we should wait for the helicopter.'

Jenna couldn't breathe. If Ryan agreed to wait for the helicopter then Lexi might drown. But if Ryan went down there—if he put himself at risk for her daughter and the two boys…

'You're wasting time, Nick.' His eyes flickered to hers and for a brief moment the connection was there. 'It will be all right. Trust me.'

And she did. Although why she should be so ready to trust a man she'd known for weeks when a man she'd known for years had let her down, she didn't understand. But life wasn't always easy to understand, was it? Some things happened without an explanation.

'What can I do?' Her mouth was so dry she could hardly form the words. 'How can I help?'

'You can stay there, away from the edge.'

Nick caught his arm. 'Ryan—'

'I'm going to abseil down, and I want you to lower the rest of my pack.' He adjusted his harness for a final time and held out his hand. 'Do you have a radio for me?'

Nick gave up arguing, but his face was white and his eyes flickered between the rising tide and the sky, obviously looking for a helicopter. Hoping.

Jenna felt helpless. 'I want to do something. If the boy is badly injured you'll need help. I can abseil down, too—'

Ryan didn't spare her a glance. 'You'll stay here.'

'It's my daughter down there.'

'That's why you're staying up here. You'll be too busy worrying about her to be any use to me.'

'Don't patronise me.' Anger spurting through her veins, Jenna picked up a harness. 'You need me down there, Ryan. Two of them are in the water, one of them injured, and one of them is stuck on the rock face. He could fall at any moment. You can't do this by yourself, and Lexi is just a child.'

Ryan paused. Then he looked over his shoulder, down at the jagged rocks. 'All right. This is what we'll do. I'll go down there first and do an assessment. If I need you, Nick can get you down to me. But watch my route. Have you abseiled before?'

Jenna swallowed, wishing she could tell him she'd scaled Everest four times without oxygen. 'Once. On an adventure camp when I was fifteen.'

'I love the fact that you're so honest. Don't worry—Nick can get you down there if I need you. Hopefully I won't.'

He went over the edge like someone from an action movie and Jenna blinked. Clearly there was plenty she still had to learn about Ryan, and the more she knew, the more she liked and admired him.

'I should have stopped him,' Nick muttered, and Jenna lifted an eyebrow because the idea of stopping Ryan doing something he was determined to do seemed laughable to her.

'How?'

The policeman gave a short laugh. 'Good question. Still, what Ryan doesn't know about ropes and climbing isn't worth knowing. I'm going to get this on you Jenna.' He had a harness in his hands. 'Just in case. I have a feeling he's going to need you. I can't believe I'm doing this.'

'If he's going to need me, why didn't he just say so?'

'Honestly? I'm guessing he's being protective. Either that or he doesn't want any of us to know how easy it is.' With a weak grin, Nick adjusted the harness and glanced at her face. Jenna wondered if he knew that there was something going on between them or whether he was matchmaking like the others.

Ryan's voice crackled over the radio. 'Nick, do you read me? I need you to lower that rope to me, over.'

'What he really needs is a miracle,' Nick muttered, lowering one end of a rope down to Ryan and securing the other end to a rock. 'That should keep the boy steady while Ryan finds out what's going on. I hope he does it quickly. There's a storm coming. Great timing. Can today get any worse?'

Only an hour earlier she'd been lying on the grass on Ryan's cliffs, bathed in sunshine and happiness.

Eyeing the rolling black clouds, Jenna approached the edge cautiously. Peering over the side, she caught her breath. Here, the cliff face was vertical. The rocks plunged downwards, the edges ragged and sharp as sharks' teeth, ready to razor through the flesh of the unwary. Her stomach lurched, and the sheer terror of facing that drop almost swallowed her whole.

'I can't believe they thought they could jump down there,' she said faintly, biting her lip as she saw Ryan attaching the rope to a boy clinging halfway down. Then her gaze drifted lower and she saw Lexi's small figure, crouched on an exposed rock at the bottom. The girl had her arms around a boy's shoulders, holding him out of the water, straining with the effort as the sea boiled and foamed angrily around them, the level of the water rising with each incoming wave.

Watching the waves lick hungrily at her daughter, Jenna felt physically sick. 'That boy is going to be under the water in another few minutes. Lexi isn't strong enough to pull him out. And she isn't going to be strong enough to keep herself out.' Feeling completely helpless, she turned to Nick. 'Get me down there now. Don't wait for Ryan to talk to you. He has his hands full. I can help—I know I can.'

'I'm not risking another person unless I have to. It's bad enough Ryan going down there, but at least he knows what he's doing. You have no cliff rescue skills—'

'I'm her mother,' Jenna said icily. 'That counts for a great deal, believe me. Get me down there, Nick.'

He slid his fingers into the collar of his jacket, easing the pressure. 'If someone has to go it should probably be me.'

'You need to stay up here to co-ordinate with the coast-guard. I don't know anything about that—I wouldn't have a

clue.' Jenna glanced down again and saw that Ryan had secured the boy and was now abseiling to the bottom of the cliff.
He landed on shiny deadly rock just as another enormous
wave rushed in and swamped both teenagers.

Instantly Ryan's voice crackled over the radio. 'Get Jenna
down here, Nick. It's an easy abseil—'

Easy? Torn between relief and raw terror, Jenna switched
off her brain. To think was to panic, and she couldn't afford
to panic. Her daughter had climbed down there, she reminded
herself as she leaned backwards and did as Nick instructed.
All the same, there was a moment when her courage failed
her and she thought she was going to freeze on the black for-
bidding rock.

'Just take it steady, Jen.' Ryan's voice came from below
her, solid and secure. 'You're nearly there.'

To stop would be to disappoint him as well as risk lives,
so Jenna kept going, thinking to herself that if he genuinely
thought this was easy she wouldn't want to do a difficult
abseil. The cliff fell away sharply and she went down slowly,
listening to Ryan's voice from below her, thinking of Lexi and
not of the drop, or of the man who had died when his rope
was severed. As her feet finally touched the rocks strong
hands caught her. Ryan's hands.

He unclipped the rope and the sea immediately swamped
her feet. If he hadn't clamped an arm around her waist she
would have stumbled under the sudden pressure of the water.
As it was, the cold made her gasp. Above her the cliff face
towered, blocking out the last of the sunshine, revealing only
ominous clouds in the chink of sky above. Here, in the slit of
the rock, it was freezing.

She guessed that if the helicopter didn't manage to get to
them soon, then it would be too late. The weather would close
in and make flying impossible.

And then what?

'The tide is coming in—Ryan, I can't hold his head any longer—' Lexi's voice came from behind them and Jenna turned, her stomach lurching as she saw the blood on her daughter's tee shirt.

'It's not mine.' Lexi read her mind and gave a quick shake of her head. 'It's Matt's. His legs—both of them, I think. He jumped in and hit rock under the surface. I didn't know what to do—he's too heavy. Mummy, do something!'

Mummy. She hadn't heard 'Mummy' since Lexi was about six, and it sent strength pouring back through her rubbery legs.

'Just hold on, Lexi.' Her voice was firm and confident, and Ryan gave her a brief smile and released her, checking that she was steady on her feet before crossing the rocks to the two teenagers.

'You're a total star, Lexi. I just need you to hold on for another minute. Can you do that?' He ripped equipment out of the rucksack as he spoke, and Jenna saw Lexi swallow as she stared up at him.

'Yes.'

'Good. We're going to get him out of the water now, and you're going to help.' Ryan had a rope in his hand. 'Just do everything I say.'

Jenna saw the fierce light of determination in her daughter's eyes—saw the faith and trust in her expression as she looked at Ryan.

Gone was the child who moaned when she couldn't get a mobile phone signal.

Jenna's flash of pride lasted only seconds as she saw another huge wave bearing down on them.

She saw Ryan glance at Lexi and then back towards her, trying to make a decision.

Jenna made the decision for him. 'Hold onto the children!' She slithered towards the rock face and managed to get a grip just as the wave rose in height and started to break. With a ferocious roar it crashed onto the rocks with an explosion of white froth, as if determined to claim its prize. Jenna clung, feeling the water pull at her and then retreat.

Wiping salt water from her face, she looked over her shoulder and saw that Ryan had his hands on Lexi's shoulders, holding her. As soon as the wave receded he turned his attention to Matt. The boy was moaning softly, his body half in and half out of the water.

'My legs—I can't put any weight—'

'Yeah—we're going to help you with that.' Ryan glanced around him, judging, coming up with a plan. 'If we can get him clear of the water and onto that rock higher up, that should give us at least another ten minutes before the tide hits us again. Enough time to check the damage and give him some pain relief.' He spoke into the radio, telling Nick what he was doing and listing the equipment he needed. 'While they're sorting that out, I'm going to get a rope on you, Matt.'

'Just leave me.' His face white with pain, the boy choked the words out. 'I don't want anyone to drown because of me.'

'No one is drowning today.' Ryan looped the rope under the boy's shoulders and secured it to a shaft of rock that jutted out of the cliff. Then he did the same to Lexi. 'The rope is going to hold both of you if another wave comes before we're done. We're going to get you out of the water, Matt. Then I'm going to give you something for the pain.' He questioned the boy about the way he'd landed, about his neck, about the movement in his limbs.

Jenna wondered why he didn't give the boy painkillers first, but then she saw another wave rushing down on them and realised that the boy was only minutes from drowning. Rope or no rope, if Ryan couldn't lift him clear of the water the boy was dead.

As the wave swamped all four of them Jenna held her

breath and gripped the rock tightly. The tide was coming in. They didn't have much time.

'What can I do?'

'Do you see that narrow ledge just under the waterline? Stand on it. I need you to hold his body steady so that we move him as little as possible.' As a precaution, Ryan put a supportive collar around Matt's neck.

Jenna stepped into the water, gritting her teeth as the ice-cold sea turned her legs numb. If she felt this cold, how must the children be feeling? She steadied Matt's body, her hands firm. 'I'm ready.'

'I'm going to lift—try not to let his legs drag against the rocks.'

Using nothing but brute strength and hard muscle, Ryan hauled the boy out of the water. Matt's screams echoed around the narrow chasm, bouncing off the rocks and adding to the deadly feel of the place.

Her heart breaking for him, Jenna gritted her teeth, wanting to stop but knowing they couldn't. They had to get him clear of the water. He'd already been in there too long. Even as Ryan lifted him she saw the terrible gashes on the boy's legs and knew they were dealing with serious injuries. Blood mixed with the water, and as they laid him flat on the rock Matt was white-faced, his lips bloodless.

'Shaft of femur—both legs.' Now that he could see the damage, Ryan worked swiftly, checking for other injuries and then examining the wound. 'Jenna, we need to control the bleeding on his left leg and cover that wound. Get me pads and a broad bandage out of the rucksack. I'm going to give him some Ketamine. Matt, this will help with the pain.'

Matt groaned. 'I'm going to die. I know I am—'

'You're not going to die.' Seeing Lexi's horrified look, Jenna spoke firmly, and Ryan gave the boy's shoulder a quick squeeze.

'No one is dying on my shift,' he said easily, and Matt made a sound that was halfway between a sob and a moan.

'If the pain doesn't kill me, my mum will.'

Jenna closed her hand over his, checking that Lexi was safely out of the water. 'Your mum won't kill you,' she said huskily. 'She's just going to be relieved you're OK.'

Ryan's gaze flickered to hers and she read his mind.

Matt was far from OK. He had two fractured femurs and he was still losing blood. Knowing that she had to help, Jenna let go of the boy's hand and dug into the rucksack, finding what she needed. Thinking clearly now, she ripped open the sterile dressings and talked to her daughter. 'Lexi? Do you have your digital camera with you?'

'What?' Soaked through and shivering, Lexi stared at her mother as though she were mad. 'Matt's bleeding half to death here and you want me to take a photo of the view?'

'He's not bleeding to death.' Taking her cue from Ryan, Jenna kept her voice calm. 'I don't want you to take the view. I want you to take a picture of Matt's legs. It will help the ER staff.'

'Good thinking.' Ryan injected the Ketamine. '*Do* you have your camera, Lex?'

'Yes—yes. But…' Baffled, Lexi cast a glance at Matt and rose to her feet, holding the rocks so that she didn't slip. She was wearing jeans, and the denim was dark with seawater. 'In my jacket pocket. What do you want me to do?'

'Take several pictures of the wounds. I'll do it, if you like.' Jenna was worried about her daughter seeing the extent of the injuries, but Lexi just gritted her teeth and pointed her digital camera. She took several photos and checked them quickly.

'OK. It's done.'

'Good.' Now that the pictures were taken, Jenna covered the wounds. 'It saves the receiving team in the hospital from removing the dressings from his legs to see what's going on.'

'Oh. I get it.' Several shades paler than she'd been a moment earlier, Lexi nodded. 'What else can I do?'

'Stay out of reach of the waves,' Ryan said immediately, his hands on Jenna's as they packed the wound, using a bandage to hold it in place. 'Any change—tell me. Jen, I'm going to splint both legs together.'

They worked as a team, Jenna following his instructions to the letter. It didn't matter that she'd never done anything like this before because his commands were clear and precise. Do this. Do that. Put your hands here—

Later, she'd look back on it and wonder how he could have been so sure about everything, but for now she just did as she was told.

Checking the pulse in both Matt's feet, she nodded to Ryan. 'His circulation is good in both legs.'

'Right. Lex, take this for me.' Ryan passed his radio to Lexi, freeing up his hands. Then he turned back to the boy. 'Matt, you've broken both your legs. I'm going to put a splint on them because that will reduce the bleeding and it will help the pain.' He looked towards Lexi. 'Logan should be up there by now. Make contact and tell Nick I need a towel.'

A towel? Glancing at the water around them, Jenna wondered if he'd gone mad, and then reminded himself that everything he'd done so far had been spot-on.

Worried that all this was too much for Lexi, Jenna was about to repeat the instructions but Lexi was already working the radio. Doing everything she'd been asked to do, she talked to Nick and relayed messages back and forth, copying the radio style she'd heard Ryan use.

'Dr McNeil is there. He wants to know what you need.'

'I'll have a Sager splint, if he has one, otherwise any traction splint. And oxygen. And ask Nick if we have an ETA on the helicopter.'

'Sager?' Jenna handed him a Venflon and Ryan slid the

cannula into the vein in Matt's arm as smoothly as if he was working in a state-of-the-art emergency unit, not a chasm in the rocks.

'It's an American splint. I prefer it.'

'They're lowering it down now. I'll get it.' One eye on the waves, Lexi picked her way across the slippery rocks like a tightrope walker and reached for the rucksack that had been lowered on the end of a rope.

Watching the boiling cauldron of water lapping angrily at her daughter's ankles, Jenna prayed that she wouldn't slip. Pride swelled inside her and she blinked rapidly, forcing herself to concentrate on her part of the rescue. 'Is it possible to apply a splint in these conditions with just the two of us?'

'I can do it in two and a half minutes, and it will make it easier to evacuate him by helicopter.' Ryan took the rucksack Lexi handed him and opened it. Using the towel, he dried Matt's legs and then opened the bag containing the splint. In a few swift movements he'd removed, unfolded and assembled the splint. 'OK, that's ready.' He positioned it between Matt's legs, explaining what he was doing.

Hearing the sound of a helicopter overhead, Jenna looked up, relief providing a much-needed flood of warmth through her body. 'Oh, thank goodness—they're here.'

Ryan didn't look up. 'They can take Jamie off first. By the time they have him in the helicopter Matt will be ready.' He wrapped the harness around the boy's ankles. 'Lexi, tell Nick.' He was treating the girl like an adult, showing no doubt in her ability to perform the tasks he set.

Without faltering Lexi spoke into the radio again, obviously proud to have something useful to do.

Jenna helped Ryan with the splint. 'How much traction do you apply?'

'Generally ten per cent of the patient's body weight per fractured femur.' Eyeing Matt's frame, Ryan checked the amount of traction on the scale. 'I'm making an educated guess.'

The noise of the helicopter increased, and Jenna watched in awe as the winchman was lowered into the narrow gap between the cliffs. In no time he had a harness on Jamie and was lifting him towards the helicopter.

'At least there's no wind.' Ryan secured straps around Matt's thighs until both legs were well supported.

Staggered by the speed with which he'd applied the splint, Jenna took Matt's hand. 'How are you doing?'

'It feels a bit better,' Matt muttered, 'but I'm not looking forward to going up in that helicopter.'

'You're going to be fine. They're experts.' Ryan watched as the winchman was lowered again, this time with a stretcher. 'We're going to get you on board, Matt, and then I'll give you oxygen and fluid on our way to hospital. Once we're on dry land, we can make you comfortable.'

Jenna looked at him, his words sinking home.

Ryan was leaving them.

She gave herself a mental shake. Of course he had to go with the casualty. What else? But she couldn't stop the shiver, and her palms dug a little harder into the grey slippery rock as she kept hold.

Ryan helped the winchman transfer Matt onto the stretcher. They had a conversation about the injury, the loss of blood— Jenna knew they were deciding whether it was best to have a doctor on board. The winchman was a paramedic, but still—

She watched as Matt was lifted slowly out of the narrow gap between the rocks, the winchman steadying the stretcher.

Once he was safely inside the helicopter, Ryan turned to Jenna.

Seeing the indecision on his face, she didn't hesitate.

'You should go! He might need you. You have to leave us here while you get him to hospital.'

Ryan's face was damp with seawater, his hair soaked, his jaw tense. 'I can't see any other way.' Already the winchman was being lowered for the final time.

Jenna lifted her chin. 'You're wasting time. We'll be fine, Ryan. We'll climb a little higher and the helicopter will be back for us soon. They're ready for you.' She watched, dry-mouthed, as the winchman landed on the rocks. 'Go.' To make it easier for both of them, she turned away and picked her way over the rocks to Lexi.

The girl was shivering, although whether it was from the cold or shock, Jenna didn't know.

She was shivering, too.

'They'll be back for us ever so quickly. You did so well, Lexi. I was so proud of you.' She wrapped her arms around her daughter and rubbed the girl's back, trying to stop the shivering. 'Oh, you're soaked through, you poor thing. How long have you been in that water? You must be freezing.'

'Is Matt going to die, Mum?' Lexi's teeth were chattering and her long hair fell in wet ropes around her shoulders. 'There was so much blood—'

'That's because the seawater made it seem like more.' Jenna's protective instincts flooded to the surface as she heard the fear in Lexi's voice and decided this was one of those times when it was best to be economical with the truth. 'He isn't going to die. He is seriously injured, and he's going to be spending quite a bit of time in hospital, but he'll be all right, I'm sure. Largely thanks to you. How did you do it, Lexi? How did you climb down here?' Her stomach tightened at the thought.

'He was just lying there, Mum. I had to do something.'

Jenna hugged her tightly. 'You saved his life.'

'Not me. Ryan.' Lexi hugged her back. 'Did you see him come down that cliff face, Mum? It was like watching one of those special forces movies. Commandos or something.'

'Yes, I saw.' Jenna closed her eyes, trying to wipe out the

image of her daughter negotiating those deadly, slippery rocks without a rope.

'And he knew exactly what to do—'

'Yes.'

Lexi gave a sniff and adjusted her position on the rock. 'He's so cool. And you were good, too, Mum. I've never seen you work before. I didn't know you were so—I dunno—so great.'

Jenna smiled weakly. 'It's amazing what you can do when the tide is coming in.'

'You and Ryan get on well together. You look like—a team.'

Jenna stilled. Had Lexi guessed that her relationship with Ryan had deepened into something more? 'We are a team. A professional team,' she said firmly, and Lexi lifted her head.

'Do you like him, Mum?'

Oh, no, not now. 'Of course I like him. I think he's an excellent doctor and—'

'That wasn't what I was asking!' Lexi's teeth were chattering. 'He was really worried about you. You should have seen the look on his face when he had to decide whether to hang onto me or you. He never took his eyes off you. If you'd been swept into the water he'd have been in there after you. What's going on?'

This was the perfect time to say something.

Jenna licked her lips. 'Do you like Ryan, sweetheart?'

'Oh, yes. And I like Evanna and the kids, and Fraser. Loads of people, actually. I never thought this place would be so cool.' Lexi clung tighter. 'I've got used to it here, Mum. I like Glenmore. And do you know the best thing?'

Ryan, Jenna thought. He was the best thing. 'Tell me the best thing for you.'

'The fact that it's just the two of us. I love that.'

Just the two of us.

Jenna swallowed down the words she'd been about to speak. How could she say them now?

Lexi buried her face in Jenna's shoulder. 'Dad was awful to you. I see that now. He didn't even tell you stuff face to face. He just let you find out.'

'I expect he did what he thought was best.' Burying her own needs, Jenna watched as the sea level rose. 'Don't think about it now.' They needed to climb higher, she thought numbly, glancing upwards with a sinking feeling in her stomach. Now that the immediate crisis was over, the impossibility of it overwhelmed her.

'I want to talk about it, Mum!' Lexi seemed to have forgotten her surroundings. 'You're always protecting me, but I want the truth.'

Shivering, wet, chilled to the bone, Jenna tried to stop her teeth from chattering as she searched for the right thing to say. 'Dad— He— Actually, Lex, I don't know what happened with your dad. The truth is that sometimes the people we love disappoint us. But I'm not going to do that. I will always be here for you. Always. You'll have a home with me always.' She smoothed the girl's soaking hair. 'Even when you're off at university, or travelling the world, you'll still have a home with me.'

If they survived.

If they didn't both drown in this isolated, godforsaken gash in the cliff face.

'Dad just acted like he didn't have a family—' Lexi's voice jerked. 'I mean, he made you sell the house so that he could have the money, and he didn't even want me to go and stay with him this summer. That's why we came up here, isn't it? You made it impossible for me to get back there, so I wouldn't find out the truth. But when I rang him he told me it wasn't convenient for me to come—he didn't want me around, and that's why we came up here.'

Jenna stroked her daughter's soaking hair, smoothing it away from her face. 'I don't know what's going on in your dad's head right now, sweetheart, but I do know he loves you. You need to give him time to sort himself out.'

'He loves me as long as I don't mess up his new life.' Lexi scrubbed tears away with her hand. 'I'm sorry I was so difficult. I'm sorry I made it hard for you.'

'You didn't. It always would have been hard. Having you is what's kept me going. Having you is the best thing that ever happened in my life.' With a flash of relief, Jenna saw the helicopter and drew Lexi back against the rock face. 'Right. They're going to get us out of here. You go first.'

Lexi clung to her mother. 'I don't want to leave you here—'

'I'll be right behind you, I promise.'

As Lexi was clipped onto the rope and lifted into the helicopter Jenna had a few moments alone on the rock.

Looking at the swirling, greedy sea, she knew that she was facing the most difficult decision of her life. She thought back to the moment when Ryan had been forced to choose between holding her and holding her daughter and the injured boy. That was life, wasn't it? It was full of tough decisions. Things were rarely straightforward and every decision had a price.

If she told Lexi about her relationship with Ryan, she'd threaten her daughter's security and happiness. And what could she offer Ryan? He wanted a family. Babies. Even if she was able to have more children, how could she do that to Lexi?

There was no choice to make because it had already been made for her.

Clinging to the rock, Jenna watched Lexi pulled to safety inside the helicopter, the seawater mingling with her tears.

CHAPTER NINE

OVERNIGHT, Lexi became a heroine.

As word spread of her daring climb down the cliffs to save Matt, Jenna couldn't walk two steps along the bustling quay without being stopped and told how proud she must be feeling. Every time she opened her front door there was another gift lying there waiting for them. Fresh fruit. Cake. Chocolate. Hand-knitted socks for Lexi—

'What am I expected to do with these? They're basically disgusting!' Back to her insouciant teenage self, Lexi looked at them in abject horror. 'I wouldn't be seen dead in them. Who on earth thinks I'll look good in purple and green? Just shoot me now.'

'You'll wear them,' Jenna said calmly, and Lexi shuddered.

'How to kill off your love-life. If I'd known there was going to be this much fuss I would have let Matt drown.' She grabbed a baseball cap and pulled it onto her head, tipping the brim down. 'If this is how it feels to be a celebrity, I don't want any of it. Two people took photos of me yesterday, and I've got a spot on my chin!'

Jenna smiled at the normality of it. It helped. There was an ache and an emptiness inside her, far greater than she'd felt after Clive had left. One pain had been replaced by another. 'Ryan rang.' She kept her voice casual. 'He thought you'd want to know that Matt's surgery went well and he's definitely not in any danger. The surgeons said that if he'd lost any more blood he might have died, so you really are the hero of the hour.'

'It wasn't me, it was Ryan.' Obviously deciding that being a heroine had its drawbacks, Lexi stuffed her iPod into her pocket and strolled towards the door. 'I'm meeting Fraser on the beach. At least that way I might be able to walk five centimetres. And, no, I'm not wearing those socks.'

'You can wear them in the winter.'

'Any chance of us moving back to London before the weather is cold enough for socks?' But, despite the sarcasm, there was humour in her eyes and Lexi gave Jenna a swift hug and a kiss. 'What are you doing today?'

'Nothing much. Just pottering. I might go for a walk.' To the lighthouse, to tell Ryan that their relationship had to end.

Jenna watched as Lexi picked up her phone and strolled out of the house, hips swaying to the music which was so loud that Jenna could hear it even without the benefit of the earphones.

Her daughter was safe, she thought. That was all that mattered. Safe and settled. And as for the rest—well, she'd cope with it.

Ryan was standing on the cliffs, staring out over the sea, when he heard the light crunch of footsteps on the path. Even without turning he knew it was her. And he knew what she'd come to say.

Bracing himself, he turned. 'I didn't think you'd be coming over today. I assumed you'd be resting—that's why I rang instead of coming round.'

'We appreciated the call. We've both been thinking about Matt all night.' She was wearing jeans and her hair blew in the wind. She looked like a girl, not a mother. 'Lexi has gone for a walk and I wanted to talk to you.'

He wanted to stop her, as if not giving her the chance to

say the words might change things. But what was the point of that? Where had denial ever got him? 'Are you all right after yesterday? No ill effects?'

'No. We were just cold. Nothing that a hot bath didn't cure. Ryan—'

'I know what you're going to say, Jenna.'

'You do?'

'Of course. You want to end it.'

She took so long to answer that he wondered if he'd got it wrong, and then she made a sound that was somewhere between a sigh and a sob. 'I have to. This just isn't a good time for me to have a new relationship. I have to think of Lexi. She's found out just how selfish her dad has been—she feels rejected and unimportant—if I put my happiness before hers, I'll be making her feel as though she matters to no one. I can't do that. She says she likes the fact that it's just the two of us. Our relationship is her anchor. It's the one thing that hasn't changed. I don't want to threaten that.'

'Of course you don't.' Ryan felt numb and strangely detached. 'I love you—you know that, don't you?'

'Yes.' Her feet made no sound in the soft grass as she walked towards him. 'And I love you. And that's the other reason I can't do this. You want children. You deserve children, Ryan. I'm thirty-three. I have no idea whether I can even have another child. And even if I could—and even if Lexi accepted our relationship in time—I couldn't do that to her. She'd feel really pushed out.' The hand she placed on his arm shook. 'What am I saying? I'm talking about children and a future and you haven't even said what you want—'

'I want you.' It was the one question he had no problem answering. In a mind clouded with thoughts and memories, it was the one thing that was shiny and clear. 'Have you talked to Lexi about it at all?'

'No. No, I haven't.'

'Maybe you should.' Refusing to give up without a fight, he slid his hands into her hair and brought his mouth down on hers. The kiss was hungry and desperate, and he wondered if by kissing her he was simply making it worse for them both. He tasted her tears and lifted her head. 'Sorry. That wasn't fair of me.'

'It isn't you. It isn't your fault.' She scrubbed her palm over her cheek. 'But we're grown-ups. She's a child. This whole situation is terrible for her, and I'd do anything to change it, but I can't. The one thing I can do is not make things worse.' Her voice broke. 'She is not ready for me to have another relationship.'

'Are you telling me that you're never going to have another relationship in case it upsets Lexi?'

'One day, maybe. But not yet. It's just too soon. I won't do anything that makes this whole thing worse for her. I suppose I could hide our relationship, but I don't want to. I don't want to sneak around and live a lie. We deserve better.' Jenna lifted her fingers to her temples and shook her head. 'This is ridiculous. I may be thirty-three but I feel seventeen. And I never should have started this. I never should have hurt you—'

'You've always been honest with me, and that's all I ask.' The hopelessness of it made the moment all the more intense, and their mouths fused, their hands impatient and demanding as they took from each other. Urgent, hungry, they made love on the grass, with the call of the seagulls and the crash of the sea for company.

Aferwards they lay on the grass in silence, because there was nothing more to say.

When Jenna stood up and walked away he didn't stop her.

The following day Jenna was half an hour late to surgery because everyone had kept stopping her to ask her for the details or give her another bit of gossip. Feeling numb inside, she'd responded on automatic, her thoughts on Ryan. 'Thank you—so kind—yes, we're both fine—no permanent damage—Matt's doing well—'

The effort of keeping up a front was so exhausting that she was relieved when she finally pushed open the glass doors to the Medical Centre. Hurrying through Reception, she was caught in an enormous hug by a woman she'd never met before.

'Nurse Jenna—how can I thank you?'

'I—' Taken aback, Jenna cast a questioning glance at Janet, the receptionist, who grinned.

'That's Pam. Matt's aunt. He has four aunts living on the island, so there's going to be more where that came from.' Janet handed a signed prescription to one lady and answered the phone with her other hand. 'There's a crowd waiting for you here, Jenna.'

Matt's aunt was still hugging her tightly. 'It's thanks to your lass that our boy's alive. I heard she climbed down—and then you went down that rope after her.'

'Lexi was brave, that's true—I'm very proud of her. And Ryan. But I didn't do anything.' Embarrassed by the fuss, desperate to be on her own, Jenna eased herself away from the woman, but people still crowded around her.

'Can't believe you went down that rope—'

'Lexi climbed down without any help—'

'Anyone who says today's teenagers are a waste of space has never met a Glenmore teenager—'

'Devil's Jaws—'

'Been more deaths there than any other part of Glenmore—'

Jenna lifted a hand to her throbbing head. 'Maybe I'd rather not hear that part,' she said weakly, remembering with horrifying clarity the moment when she'd stepped over the edge of the cliff. 'I'm just so pleased Matt's going to be all right. Dr McKinley rang yesterday and the hospital said surgery went well.' After a summer on Glenmore she knew better than to bother worrying about patient confidentiality. If she didn't tell them what was going on they'd find out another way, and the information would be less reliable. 'I'm just sorry I'm late this morning. If everyone could be patient…'

'Don't give it a thought.' Kate Green, who ran the gift shop on the quay, waved a hand. 'Won't kill any of us to wait. Anything we can do to help? We're sorting out a rota to make food for Matt's family when they're back from the mainland. They won't want to be fussing with things like that.'

Jenna looked at them all—looked at their kind faces, which shone with their eagerness to support each other in times of crisis. It was impossible not to compare it to the surgery she'd worked at in London, where patients had complained bitterly if they were kept waiting more than ten minutes. In London everyone led parallel lives, she thought numbly. Here, lives were tangled together. People looked left and right instead of straight ahead. They noticed if things weren't right with the person next to them. They helped.

Someone pushed something into her hand.

Jenna opened the bag and saw two freshly baked muffins.

'My mum thought you might not have had time for breakfast. We made you these.' The child was no more than seven years old, and for Jenna it was the final straw. Too emotionally fragile to cope with the volume of kindness, she burst into tears.

'Oh, now…' Clucking like a mother hen, Kate Green urged her towards the nearest chair.

'Shock—that's what it is. It was her lass who stayed with Matt. Saved him, she did. That's a worry for any mother.'

'Tired, I expect…'

'I'm so sorry.' Struggling desperately to control herself, Jenna rummaged in her pocket for a tissue. Someone pushed one into her hand. 'Just leave me for a minute—I'll be fine.'

Oh, God, she was going to crack. Right here in public, with these kind people around her.

Evanna hurried out of her clinic, alerted by Janet. 'Jenna? Are you all right?'

Jenna blew her nose. 'Just being really stupid. And making my clinic even more behind than it is at the moment.'

'Then perhaps we can get on with it? I'm first.' Mrs Parker's crisp voice cut through the mumbling and the sympathy. 'And I've been standing on this leg for twenty minutes now. I'm too old to be kept waiting around. It isn't the first drama we've had on Glenmore and it won't be the last.'

Even the gentle Evanna gritted her teeth, but Jenna stood up, grateful to be forced into action.

'Of course, Mrs Parker. I'm so sorry. Come with me. The rest of you—' she glanced around the crowded waiting room '—I'll be as quick as I can.'

Following Mrs Parker down the corridor to her room, Jenna braced herself for a sharp rebuke and a lecture.

Instead she was given a hug. 'There, now…' Mrs Parker's voice shook slightly, and her thin fingers rubbed Jenna's back awkwardly. 'Those folks think they're helping, but they're overwhelming, aren't they? I've lived on this island all my life and there are times when I could kill the lot of them. You must feel like a crust of bread being fought over by a flock of seagulls.' With a sniff she pulled away, leaving Jenna with a lump in her throat.

'Oh, Mrs Parker—'

'Now, don't you get all sentimental on me, young lady.' Mrs Parker settled herself in the chair. 'Sentimental is all very well once in a while, but it doesn't solve problems. I'm guessing those tears have nothing to do with that foolhardy rescue or lack of sleep. Do you want to talk about it?'

Jenna blew her nose again. 'I'm supposed to be dressing your leg—'

'You're a woman. Are you telling me you can't talk and bandage a leg at the same time?'

Jenna gave a weak smile and turned her attention to work. Washing her hands, she prepared the equipment she needed. 'It's just reaction to yesterday, I'm sure. And I am a little tired. Really.'

'I'm old, not stupid. But not so old I don't remember how it feels to be confused about a man. You came here as a single mother. I'm guessing you're rethinking that now.'

Jenna's hands shook as she removed the bandage from the old lady's leg. 'No. No, I'm not rethinking that. Lexi and I are a team.'

'So you're going to let a strong, impressive man like Dr McKinley walk away from you?'

Jenna stilled. She thought about denying it and then realised it was useless. 'Does everyone know?'

Mrs Parker sighed. 'Of course. This is Glenmore. What we don't know is why you're not just booking the church. The Reverend King is quite happy to marry you, even though you've been divorced. I asked him.'

'You—?' Jenna gulped. 'Mrs Parker, you can't possibly—you shouldn't have—'

'You have a daughter. You need to keep it respectable. One bad marriage shouldn't put you off doing it again.' Mrs Parker glared at her. 'What? You think it's right, teaching that girl of yours it's all right to take up with whoever takes your fancy? You need to set an example. If you like him enough to roll around in his sheets with him, you like him enough to marry him. And he certainly likes you. There's a bet going on down at the pub that he's going to ask you to marry him. You'd better have your answer ready.'

'It would have to be no.'

Mrs Parker looked at her steadily, her customary frown absent. 'As we've been drinking tea together for almost two months now, perhaps you'd do me the courtesy of explaining why you'd say no to a man most women would kill to be with.'

Jenna didn't pause to wonder why she was talking to this woman. She needed to talk to someone, and Mrs Parker had proved to be a surprisingly good listener. 'Because of Lexi.'

She blurted it all out. Everything she was feeling. The only thing she didn't mention was Ryan's past. That wasn't hers to reveal.

Mrs Parker listened without interrupting. Only when Jenna had finished and was placing a fresh dressing on the wound did she finally speak. Her hands were folded carefully in her lap.

Age and wisdom, Jenna thought, wondering what secrets Mrs Parker had in her past. She was a girl once. A young woman. *We see them as patients, but they're people.*

'Tell me something.' The old lady looked at her in the eye. 'Do you plan to try and shield your daughter from everything that happens in life?'

Jenna swallowed. 'If I can.' Then she gave a sigh. 'No, of course not. Not everything, but—I love her. I want her to be happy.'

'Has it occurred to you that she might like a new man around the house?'

'I think it would unsettle her.' Jenna finished the bandage, concentrating on the job. 'Is that comfortable?'

Mrs Parker put her weight on her leg. 'It's perfect, as usual.' Her voice calm, she picked up her handbag. 'You're not the only one who can love, you know. And if love is wanting someone else's happiness, maybe Lexi should be thinking of yours. Maybe you should give her the chance to worry about you for a change. I want you to think about that.'

'Mrs Parker—'

'Just think about it. I'd hate to see you turning your back on something special. I'll send the next person in, shall I? Don't forget to drop in for tea when you're passing.' With a quiet smile, the dragon of Glenmore opened the door. 'I happen to know that Rev King has a date free in December. I always think a winter wedding is romantic. And I expect an invitation. I have a particularly nice coat that I haven't had reason to wear for at least two decades.'

'He rolled in a pile of something gross and now he stinks— Mum, are you listening to me? Basically, the dog is rank.' A frown on her face, Lexi helped herself to crisps from the cupboard and waved them under her mother's nose. 'Junk food alert! Time to nag!'

Her mind miles away, Jenna stared out of the window, trying to find the right way to say what needed to be said.

'On my fourth packet—' Lexi rustled the bag of crisps dramatically. 'Might add some more salt to them just to make them extra yummy—'

'Lexi…' Her strained voice caught her daughter's attention.

'What? What's wrong?'

'I—there's something I need to talk to you about. Something very adult.'

'Is it about the fact you're having sex with Ryan? Because honestly, Mum—' Lexi stuck her hand in the crisp packet '—I don't want to know the details. I mean, I love you, and I love that we talk about stuff, but I don't want to talk about that. It would feel too weird.'

Stunned, Jenna felt her face turn scarlet. 'You— I—'

'Don't get me wrong. I'm basically cool with it, Mum. I'm pleased for you.' Grinning, Lexi nibbled a crisp. 'It's nice for someone of your age to have some excitement.'

Jenna moved her lips but no sound came out.

Lexi squinted out of the window. 'Better pull it together fast, Mum, lover-boy is strolling up the path. I'll go and let him in, shall I?' She sauntered towards the door, crisps in her hand. 'Hi, Ryan. I'm glad you're here, because Mum so needs a doctor. She's acting weird. I've waved, like, five packets of crisps under her nose and she hasn't even reacted. Normally she'd be freaking out and going on about too much salt, too much fat. Today—nothing. What's the matter with her?'

'Perhaps you'd better leave us for a moment.' Ryan dropped his car keys on the table, but Lexi shook her head and plopped onto a chair by the kitchen table.

'No way. I'm fed up with being the last person to know stuff around here. If you want to get rid of me you'll have to kick me out, and that will be child abuse.'

A smile flickered at the corners of Ryan's mouth. 'Presumably that wouldn't be a good start to our relationship.'

Lexi looked at him thoughtfully. 'You've got a thing for my mum, haven't you?'

Ryan winced, and Jenna came to her senses. 'Lexi!'

'It's too late for discipline. I'm already full of crisps.' Lexi folded her arms. 'It would be great if someone around here would give me a straight answer for once. I know you like my mum, so there's no point in denying it.'

'That isn't quite how I'd describe it,' Ryan said carefully, and Jenna felt the pulse beat in her throat.

Lexi didn't pause. 'What words would you use?'

'I love your mum.' Ryan spoke the words calmly, with no hint of apology or question. 'I love her very much. But I realise that the situation is complicated.'

'What's complicated about it? She's divorced, and you—' Lexi frowned. 'Are you married or something?'

'No. I was in the past.'

'So, basically, you're free and single?' Lexi grinned cheekily. 'I missed out the "young" bit, did you notice?'

'I noticed. Remind me to punish you later.' A sardonic smile on his face, Ryan sat down at the table. 'I'm not sure what order to do this in. If you want to be part of a family that already exists, do you propose to the woman or the daughter?'

'Don't waste your time proposing to me,' Lexi said casually. 'You may be hot, but you're way too old for me. How old *are* you?'

'Thirty-six.'

Lexi shuddered. 'You'd go and die, or something, while I was still in my prime. Mind you, that has its advantages. Are you rich?'

'Lexi!' Jenna finally found her voice. 'You can't—'

'Actually, I am pretty rich. Why does that matter?' Ryan's long fingers toyed with his keys. 'Are you open to bribery and corruption?'

'Of course. I'm a teenager. The art of negotiation is an important life skill.' Lexi grabbed a grape from the fruit bowl and popped it in her mouth. 'So how big a bribe are we talking about? If I let you marry my mum you'll buy me a pink Porsche?'

Ryan grimaced. 'Not pink. Please not pink.'

Glancing between the two of them in disbelief, Jenna shook her head. 'Can we have a proper conversation?'

'We are having a proper conversation.' Lexi looked at Ryan speculatively. 'What music do you like?'

'I have eclectic tastes.'

'In other words you'll pretend to like anything I like.'

'No. But I'm sure there would be some common ground.'

'If I let you marry my mum, will you teach me to abseil?'

Jenna felt faint. 'Lexi—Ryan—for goodness' sake—'

'I don't see why not.'

'And surf?'

'Your balance was pretty impressive on those rocks, and you don't seem to mind being swamped by seawater.' Ryan gave a casual shrug and a smile touched his mouth. 'Looks like I'm going to be busy.'

'And you promise not to tell me what time to go to bed or nag me about my diet?'

'You can eat what you like and go to bed when you like.'

Lexi fiddled with his car keys. 'Do I have to call you Dad?'

'You can call me whatever you like.'

'I never thought about having another father.'

There was a long silence, and then Ryan stirred. 'How about another friend? Have you thought about having another one of those?'

Lexi gave a slow smile and stood up. 'Yeah,' she drawled huskily, 'I could go with that. I'll leave you two alone now. The thought of watching a man kiss my mum is just a bit gross. I'm taking Rebel down on the beach to wash off whatever it is he's rolled in. I reckon it's going to take me at least two hours to get him clean, and I'm going to bang the front door really loudly when I come back.' Grinning wickedly, she scooped up the lead and then walked over to Jenna. 'Say yes, Mum. You know you want to.' She glanced over her shoulder to Ryan. 'And he's pretty cool—for an older person. We're going to do OK.'

Jenna couldn't find her voice. 'Lex—'

'You're almost too old to have another baby, so you'd better not waste any time,' Lexi advised, kissing Jenna on the cheek.

Sensing Ryan's eyes on her, Jenna swallowed. 'Lexi, we won't—'

'I hope you do. Think of all the money I'd earn babysitting.' Lexi grinned. 'How much would you pay me to change nappies? I'll think about a decent rate while I'm scrubbing Rebel. See you later.' She sauntered out of the house, leaving the two of them alone.

Aware of Ryan still watching her, Jenna opened her mouth and closed it again.

He stood up and walked across to her. 'I had an unexpected visitor this morning.'

'You did?'

'The Reverend King.' There was a gleam of humour in his eyes. 'He wanted to know exactly what time we wanted the church on Christmas Eve. Apparently it's been reserved provisionally in our name. His suggestion was just before lunch, so that the entire island could then gather for food at our expense. I wondered what you thought.'

Jenna swallowed. Then she turned her head and stared into the garden, watching as Lexi put Rebel on his lead and led him through the little gate towards the beach. 'I think that life sometimes surprises you,' she said huskily. 'I think that just when you think everything is wrong, it suddenly turns out right. I think I'm lucky. What do you think?'

Ryan closed his hands over her shoulders and turned her to face him. 'I think we only have two hours before Lexi comes home.' His fingers were strong, and he held her as though he never intended to let her go. 'We should probably make the most of it. Especially if we want to make a baby before we're both too old.'

She made a sound that was somewhere between a laugh and a sob and flung her arms around his neck. 'What if I can't? What if I *am* too old? What if I can't give you a family?'

His hands gentle, he cupped her face and lowered his mouth to hers. 'Marry me and you will have given me all the family I need. You. Lexi.'

'But—'

'Sometimes we don't begin a journey knowing where it's going to end,' he said softly, resting his forehead against hers as he looked down at her. 'Sometimes we don't have all the answers. We don't know what the future holds, but we do know that whatever it is we'll deal with it. Together. The three of us. And Rebel, of course.'

The three of us.

Holding those words against her like a warm blanket, Jenna lifted her head. 'The three of us,' she whispered softly. 'That sounds good to me.'

0610 Gen Std HB

MILLS & BOON

JULY 2010 HARDBACK TITLES

ROMANCE

A Night, A Secret...A Child	Miranda Lee
His Untamed Innocent	Sara Craven
The Greek's Pregnant Lover	Lucy Monroe
The Mélendez Forgotten Marriage	Melanie Milburne
Sensible Housekeeper, Scandalously Pregnant	Jennie Lucas
The Bride's Awakening	Kate Hewitt
The Devil's Heart	Lynn Raye Harris
The Good Greek Wife?	Kate Walker
Propositioned by the Billionaire	Lucy King
Unbuttoned by Her Maverick Boss	Natalie Anderson
Australia's Most Eligible Bachelor	Margaret Way
The Bridesmaid's Secret	Fiona Harper
Cinderella: Hired by the Prince	Marion Lennox
The Sheikh's Destiny	Melissa James
Vegas Pregnancy Surprise	Shirley Jump
The Lionhearted Cowboy Returns	Patricia Thayer
Dare She Date the Dreamy Doc?	Sarah Morgan
Neurosurgeon ... and Mum!	Kate Hardy

HISTORICAL

Vicar's Daughter to Viscount's Lady	Louise Allen
Chivalrous Rake, Scandalous Lady	Mary Brendan
The Lord's Forced Bride	Anne Herries

MEDICAL™

Dr Drop-Dead Gorgeous	Emily Forbes
Her Brooding Italian Surgeon	Fiona Lowe
A Father for Baby Rose	Margaret Barker
Wedding in Darling Downs	Leah Martyn

0610 Gen Std LP

JULY 2010 LARGE PRINT TITLES

ROMANCE

Greek Tycoon, Inexperienced Mistress	Lynne Graham
The Master's Mistress	Carole Mortimer
The Andreou Marriage Arrangement	Helen Bianchin
Untamed Italian, Blackmailed Innocent	Jacqueline Baird
Outback Bachelor	Margaret Way
The Cattleman's Adopted Family	Barbara Hannay
Oh-So-Sensible Secretary	Jessica Hart
Housekeeper's Happy-Ever-After	Fiona Harper

HISTORICAL

One Unashamed Night	Sophia James
The Captain's Mysterious Lady	Mary Nichols
The Major and the Pickpocket	Lucy Ashford

MEDICAL™

Posh Doc, Society Wedding	Joanna Neil
The Doctor's Rebel Knight	Melanie Milburne
A Mother for the Italian's Twins	Margaret McDonagh
Their Baby Surprise	Jennifer Taylor
New Boss, New-Year Bride	Lucy Clark
Greek Doctor Claims His Bride	Margaret Barker

0710 Gen Std HB

MILLS & BOON

AUGUST 2010 HARDBACK TITLES

ROMANCE

The Pregnancy Shock	Lynne Graham
Falco: The Dark Guardian	Sandra Marton
One Night...Nine-Month Scandal	Sarah Morgan
The Last Kolovsky Playboy	Carol Marinelli
The Secret Spanish Love-Child	Cathy Williams
Untouched Until Marriage	Chantelle Shaw
His Prisoner in Paradise	Trish Morey
His Virgin Acquisition	Maisey Yates
Red-Hot Renegade	Kelly Hunter
What Happens in Vegas...	Kimberly Lang
Doorstep Twins	Rebecca Winters
The Cowboy's Adopted Daughter	Patricia Thayer
SOS: Convenient Husband Required	Liz Fielding
Winning a Groom in 10 Dates	Cara Colter
Inconveniently Wed!	Jackie Braun
Maid for the Millionaire	Susan Meier
Wishing for a Miracle	Alison Roberts
The Marry-Me Wish	Alison Roberts

HISTORICAL

Lord Portman's Troublesome Wife	Mary Nichols
The Duke's Governess Bride	Miranda Jarrett
Conquered and Seduced	Lyn Randal

MEDICAL™

Prince Charming of Harley Street	Anne Fraser
The Heart Doctor and the Baby	Lynne Marshall
The Secret Doctor	Joanna Neil
The Doctor's Double Trouble	Lucy Clark

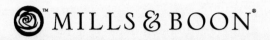

™MILLS & BOON®

0710 Gen Std LP